BODY ON BOARD

It would take about the same amount of time to drive around the harbor to the other side as it would to run across the footbridge, but after a hurried consult with Chris, we grabbed his pickup. Wyatt might need a ride to the hospital. Chris's legendary lead foot left tourists scattering as we sped across town.

We ran through Blount's, down the wooden stairs to the floating dock and up the *Garbo*'s gangway.

"Wyatt! Wyatt! Where are you?"

A strangled sound echoed from a deck somewhere above. I spotted her outside the dining salon. We raced to her. She was a wreck. Pale, shaking, crying, clutching her stomach.

"What is it, Wyatt? What's wrong?"

She straightened up and, silently, still shaking, led us into the dining room. At the head of the table, Geoffrey Bower sat motionless, wearing the same yachtsman's cap and blue blazer as the day before, his face contorted in a horrible grimace . . .

Books by Barbara Ross

CLAMMED UP

BOILED OVER

MUSSELED OUT

FOGGED INN

ICED UNDER

STOWED AWAY

EGG NOG MURDER
(with Leslie Meier and Lee Hollis)

Published by Kensington Publishing Corporation

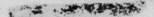

STOWED AWAY

BARBARA ROSS

𝒦

KENSINGTON BOOKS

http://www.kensingtonbooks.com

KENSINGTON BOOKS are published by

Kensington Publishing Corp.
119 West 40th Street
New York, NY 10018

All Kensington titles, imprints and distributed lines are available at special quantity discounts for bulk purchases for sales promotion, premiums, fund-raising, educational or institutional use. Special book excerpts or customized printings can also be created to fit specific needs. For details, write or phone the office of the Kensington Special Sales Manager: Kensington Publishing Corp., 119 West 40th Street, New York, NY 10018. Attn. Special Sales Department. Phone: 1-800-221-2647.

Kensington and the K logo Reg. U.S. Pat. & TM Off.

ISBN-13: 978-1-4967-0041-4
ISBN-10: 1-4967-0041-4
First Kensington Mass Market Edition: January 2018

eISBN-13: 978-1-4967-0042-1
eISBN-10: 1-4967-0042-2
First Kensington Electronic Edition: January 2018

10 9 8 7 6 5 4 3 2 1

Printed in the United States of America

This book is dedicated to the members of my writers' group: Mark Ammons, Katherine Fast, Cheryl Marceau, and Leslie Wheeler. We've laughed and cried, agreed and argued, praised and critiqued our way through twenty years. One thing I know for sure— I never would have persisted to become a published author without each of you.

Chapter 1

"Dead weight is the worst." I dropped my end of the picnic table on the flattest spot I could find.

My boyfriend, Chris, wiped his brow with a tan forearm. It was early June, but he'd been land-scaping, one of his three jobs, whenever the weather cooperated. I was lucky to have snagged him, just for the day, to help on Morrow Island.

Opening day for the Snowden Family Clambake was one short week away. While I had Chris with me, one of our projects was to move half the picnic tables out of the dining pavilion where they'd been stored for the winter and place them around Morrow Island. The spots had been picked by my parents thirty years earlier, intended to maximize the glorious views across the Gulf of Maine, or provide a cozy spot surrounded by flowers where our guests could eat lobster and toast a special occasion. Moving the tables was hard physical work. I'd been laboring under the delusion that I'd stayed in great shape during the off-season, but every grumbling muscle told me I'd been fooling myself.

I stared at our dock and the navy blue North Atlantic beyond it. "What time do you think it is?"

"One fifteen."

I pulled my phone from my pocket. Cell service didn't reach the island, but the device was keeping time. "Amazing. One fourteen and thirty seconds." Chris's ability to tell the time within minutes, day or night, based on nothing more than his internal clock, never ceased to amaze me.

Chris grinned, crinkling the skin around his green eyes. "It's a shame my only superpower, as you call it, can't earn me a dime."

I fell in step beside him as we walked back to the pavilion. "Still, it's a pretty impressive trick."

He smiled. "Glad it makes you laugh. When did Quentin say they'd be here?"

"Anytime now."

As we grabbed another picnic table, Mom stepped out of the gift shop that was tucked in a corner of the building. She hadn't worked on the island in six years—since the day my dad had been diagnosed with the cancer that killed him—but this season she'd already given notice at Linens and Pantries, the big box store where she worked, she'd be taking the summer off to run the Snowden Family Clambake gift shop. Seeing her petite, blond figure in the gift shop entryway, in a cardigan, cotton dress, and tennies brought a wave of nostalgia for the island summers of my childhood. People say I look like her, and they're mostly right.

"What time are they coming?" she asked.

"Soon," I answered. "Quentin's usually right on time."

"Be sure to call me as soon as they get here." She gave us a smile and turned back toward the gift shop.

Quentin Tupper was a family friend, a mentor, and as a result of an investment made to rescue Morrow Island from foreclosure the previous summer, a partner in the Snowden Family Clambake Company. He was also a major proponent, perhaps the most vocal proponent, of fixing up, rather than tearing down, the old mansion that sat on the island's highest peak. Windsholme had been built by my mother's ancestors with money earned shipping ice from New England to warm places like Calcutta and Havana. It was a formidable house, architecturally significant, as Quentin kept reminding us, but it had been abandoned as a dwelling place in the 1920s and damaged in a fire last summer. I understood my mother's love for and loyalty to the place, but I couldn't think of a single, practical reason for repairing it.

It wasn't about practical, Quentin hastened to add whenever the subject came up. It was about history, and architecture, and art. To move the discussion along he'd found an architect, an expert in early examples of Shingle-style homes in Maine, and today he was bringing her to Morrow Island to walk through Windsholme and offer her educated opinion.

Her name was Wyatt Jayne and I'd researched

her on the Internet. She had both architecture and landscape design degrees from Harvard and a string of academic articles and stories in glossy magazines featuring breathtaking photos of homes she'd renovated. While I was against spending the money on Windsholme, I had to admit Quentin had found a highly qualified person. At least on paper.

"Ahoy!"

The *Flittermouse*, Quentin Tupper's sailboat, motored into our dock. A slender woman stood on the deck behind Quentin. She wore large dark glasses and a scarf over her head, Jackie Kennedy style.

Chris ran to help them in. My mother came out of the gift shop and walked with me to the dock. Quentin threw Chris the lines and turned back to help his guest. Her dress, an elegantly cut shift in bright pastels, wasn't built for stepping off a sailboat. As Quentin handed her off to Chris, she fell into his arms. He danced a two-step before setting her down carefully on the wide planks.

"Whoa, thank you!" She smiled her approval at Chris, who smiled back.

"No trouble."

Quentin disembarked immediately behind her. He was a big man, sandy haired, and dressed as always in his uniform of khakis, tailored blue cotton shirt, and boat shoes, sans socks. Ten years older than me, he was forty-one to my thirty-one.

"Hullo," he said, beginning the introductions. "Wyatt, this is Jacqueline Snowden, the owner of the island and its magnificent home, her daughter, Julia

Snowden, and Chris Durand, a friend of the family."
The woman took off her sunglasses and kerchief as
Quentin continued. "Snowdens, this is—"

"I know exactly who she is," I cut him off.

"Julia Snowden!" the woman cried.

"Hello, Susan."

"What a funny coincidence. I had no idea. All the
paperwork Quentin sent me said 'Jacqueline Snowden.' I never put two and two together," she said.

"Neither did I. Especially because Quentin told
me your name was Wyatt."

"It's Susan Wyatt Jayne. I use Wyatt profession-
ally."

"You two know each other?" Quentin couldn't
have looked more delighted.

I gave him a tight-lipped smile. "We went to
school together."

Wyatt nodded her agreement. "We were a pair,
weren't we? I was editor of the yearbook and Julia
was editor of the newspaper. I was captain of the
debate team and she was—" Susan looked around,
suddenly out of parallels.

"On the debate team," I filled in helpfully.

"An alternate on the debate team," Wyatt corrected, once and apparently still a stickler for detail.
"I heard you'd gone to business school. We all
expected so much from you. We thought you'd be
running Wall Street by now."

"Yes, well." I looked down at my jeans and work
boots, covered in dirt from a day of hard physical
labor. "It hasn't turned out that way."

"I can't wait to hear all about it." Wyatt grabbed me by the arm and then pivoted to my mother, extending her hand. "Jacqueline. May I call you Jacqueline? What an honor and a privilege it is to view this magnificent home."

"We hope it will pique your interest sufficiently that you'll do more than view it." My mother gave Quentin a conspiratorial smile.

Wyatt turned to Chris. "And what is your role?"

Quentin jumped in. "Chris is a skilled home renovator who aided me in my initial assessment of the damage to Windsholme. He helped me believe it could be brought back to its former glory." Quentin paused and cleared his throat. "And Chris is a particular friend of Julia's."

That last statement caused Wyatt to give Chris another look. I watched her take him in, from the tousled light brown hair, to the arresting green eyes, the dimpled chin, the broad shoulders, and the muscled chest barely disguised by the navy T-shirt.

"Indeed," Wyatt said.

I was used to the reaction. Chris was, if anything, "too handsome for his own good," in my mother's early-on assessment. He'd won her over, eventually, and it didn't look like he was going to have to work hard to capture Wyatt's approval either. This despite his jeans and work boots, as dirty as my own. Or maybe because of them.

"Shall we see the house?" Quentin suggested.

We walked up from the dock to the wide, grassy plateau that had been known as the great lawn when Windsholme was built, a place for genteel games of croquet and badminton. It still served some of those functions, with a volleyball net and a boccie court, but now it also housed the warren of connected buildings—dining pavilion, gift shop, bar, and kitchen—that formed the heart of the clambake operation. I'd seen photographs of Windsholme in its prime and I knew the impression it must have made on people as they gazed up from the lawn.

Now the view was a decidedly mixed bag. The old rose garden and its surrounding hedges were long gone. The part of the lawn that once stretched between Windsholme and the playhouse, a miniature version of the mansion, had gone to woods. Most disturbing was the house itself. For ninety years it had received the minimum of maintenance required to keep it standing. Then, last summer, fire had destroyed its central staircase and burned a hole in the roof. That hole, along with the huge window over the stairs, and the windows on either side, had been covered with boards to keep out the winter while my family decided what to do. The entire house was cordoned off with a bright orange hazard fence, designed to keep curious clambake guests from stumbling into the property and falling through the floor. Windsholme looked like an heiress whose photo had been snapped mid-kidnapping—disheveled, eyes and mouth taped shut, and bound at the ankles. I wanted to cry every time I looked at her. And not, as people supposed, because I'd been there when the fire started, but because the house looked so sad, so wounded.

At the bottom of the stone front steps, Wyatt

paused and looked up. She didn't move for a full minute, taking in Windsholme's beautiful lines. "Hmm," she said in a tone I couldn't read. "Hmmm."

We let ourselves in to the house through the French doors to the dining room, since the front door now led to a burned-out hole in the floor. We entered into the beautifully proportioned room. There was enough light to see the hand-painted mural, the oak wainscoting, and the stone fireplace, all damaged by soot and smelling of woodsmoke, but otherwise okay.

In the low light, Wyatt examined the mural intently. "Ridley?"

Quentin nodded. "Attributed. It's unsigned."

Wyatt pulled a smartphone from her big leather bag and turned on the flashlight, training the light along the chair rail. "Shame," she said, when she'd walked the three walls the mural covered. "You're right. No signature."

"Wait until you get a load of this." Quentin stepped through a small galley next to the fireplace and pushed open the swinging door that led to the balcony surrounding the two-story kitchen in the basement. The wooden cabinets lining the balcony on all four sides were intact. There were glass-fronted cabinets for china and crystal, drawers for silver, cupboards for table linens. The contents were long gone, dispersed along with the family fortune during the 1920s. The kitchen below was empty except for a soapstone sink, iron stove, and a wooden icebox. Wyatt snapped photos like crazy.

When she was done, Quentin led us back through the dining room. He opened the door to the center hall and pointed to the burned-out floor. "No way to get through," he said. "If you want to see the rooms on the other side, we have to go outside and come in again."

Wyatt stared at the charred hallway, lips pursed in a hard, straight line. "Is there any way to get upstairs?"

"Back stairs," Chris said, turning around to lead us the other way, to the servants' stairway off the kitchen.

"Interesting," Wyatt said as we entered the narrow passageway. "Lots of these Maine island summer houses were considered to be rustic, casual retreats for the homeowners and a bit of a break for the staff. People mixed more freely. Not socially, but it wasn't a big deal to see a maid on the front stairs. This house, on the other hand, is designed to keep interactions between staff and the family to a minimum. More like Newport or Bar Harbor than a wild island."

It was the most she'd said since we'd been in the house, but I didn't know how to interpret it. Was the house's formality a good or bad thing?

We looked at the master bedroom, which ran from the front to the back of the house, with its two adjacent bathrooms.

"Original?" Wyatt asked.

Chris answered. "The house was built with indoor plumbing."

"Unusual for the period," Wyatt said. She pulled a leather-bound journal from her bag and made a note.

"Especially on an island," Chris agreed.

"You say it's attributed to Henry Gilbert?" Wyatt asked. I didn't miss the "attributed." She pointed to the large steam shower and leaned in to whisper something to Quentin, bringing her lips so close to his ear, he must have felt her breath.

Unless I was very much mistaken, she was wasting her efforts with Quentin. He lived alone in houses all over the world, including the modern marble and glass edifice across from Morrow Island on Westclaw Point that I called his Fortress of Solitude. He was disinclined to let anyone close, but if he had chosen a romantic partner, I was pretty sure it wouldn't be anyone of Wyatt's gender.

"And the grounds are, uh, attributed to students of Frederick Law Olmsted." I repeated to her rumors that had been repeated to me all my life. I'd never thought to question them, but now I did, as Wyatt furrowed her brow and wrote in her notebook. Perhaps things would go my way in the argument with Mom and Quentin. Perhaps Windsholme was not worth saving after all.

In the attic, Wyatt turned her charm on Chris. "Will you look at this?" She pointed to the place where the eaves were joined to the floor joists. "Pegs."

Chris nodded. "The house was probably built by

men who had more experience working on ships than houses. There wouldn't have been enough construction back then for the trades to be separate."

"Interesting."

Did she have attic dust in her eyes or was she batting her eyelashes at Chris? Did women really do that? Unlike Quentin, Chris had been all too susceptible to pretty women's charms, as the string of ex-girlfriends I constantly ran into in the harbor reminded me. Or at least he had been, until me. His devotion made me feel warm and loved. The women who constantly approached me to send him their greetings made me uneasy.

"This is it," Quentin said. "If you want to see more of the upstairs, we have to get a ladder on the outside."

Wyatt wasn't dressed for ladders. "I've got enough. Why don't you two men take me on a tour of the basement?"

"That puts us in our place," I said a few minutes later as I sat on a porch step next to Mom. She hadn't said a word during the tour.

"Really, Julia, what great insights could you have offered about the cellar?"

"None," I admitted, but I didn't like being excluded.

"What is up with you and Wyatt? You act funny around her."

"Long story," I answered.

"Long *ago* story," my mother said, "if you're

referring to something that happened at school. I hope it isn't going to be a problem."

"Of course not. If she's the right person for the job, she's the right person."

"She is," my mother said confidently. "I can feel it."

The merry band returned, appearing from around the corner of the stone foundation. Wyatt sat down on the porch step on the other side of my mother, smoothing the pastel shift.

"What do you think?" Mom asked. The spot over her nose creased with anticipation. The stakes were high for her.

Wyatt cleared her throat delicately and gave Mom a megawatt smile. "I think your project requires more research." She spoke slowly, as if weighing her words. "I want to check some sources."

"Will that take long? I know you're based in New York."

"I'm staying here in the harbor. My boyfriend is in town, waiting with his yacht for a refit at Herndon's. Can we meet tomorrow?"

Mom perked up. "My house in the harbor? Ten AM?"

"Perfect. And you all should come for dinner aboard tonight."

"Where's his boat?" Chris asked.

"At Blount's. It's called the *Garbo*."

Chris's eyebrows shot up. There'd been a mega-yacht anchored in the marina at Blount's Hotel for days. Even though we were used to seeing yachts in Busman's Harbor, its size had everyone in town talking about it.

"We'd love to come," Quentin said, apparently speaking for all of us.

"I'm sorry. I can't make it." Mom sounded regretful. "I'm babysitting." My sister Livvie and her husband had a four-month-old, and a ten-year-old who wasn't quite up to caring for her brother.

Wyatt must have been disappointed. My mom was the potential client, and therefore probably the person she most wanted to accept, but she didn't show it. "The rest of you then?"

"Sure, Julia and I would love to," Chris answered, without so much as a glance at me.

I smiled. Wyatt was attractive, but what Chris really wanted was to see that boat.

"Great!" Wyatt said with more enthusiasm than I thought the occasion required. "I'll send a text and let him know there'll be three guests for dinner. I'm sure he'll be interested to meet you, Julia. He's never met any of my school friends."

He wasn't going to tonight either.

As she pulled out her phone, Chris said, "You won't get service out here. You'll have to wait until you're closer to the harbor."

Her perfectly shaped eyebrows drew together over her pert little nose, but she put the phone away.

"I've got to get back to my house to clean up," Quentin said, though he looked as crisply turned-out as always, especially in comparison to Chris and me. I pictured his closet as yards-long racks of perfectly pressed blue, tailored shirts, rows of khaki-colored shorts and pants, and a hundred pairs of boat shoes. "Do you mind running Wyatt back to the harbor?" he asked us. "I'll sail home, get changed, and meet you in town."

"Sure. You can park at our place," Chris said, again without consulting with me. June days were long and normally we worked on the island until the sun went down, but today would be different. Even though I was annoyed, I couldn't say I didn't welcome the break.

Chapter 2

It took half an hour after Quentin left to finish our work and secure the island for the night. Since we'd begun prepping for the clambake season, I'd slept most nights in the little cottage by the dock where I'd spent my childhood summers. But tonight, because of the dinner, I'd stay in town at the studio apartment over Gus's restaurant that Chris and I had shared all winter, the closest thing I had to a home.

I undid the lines holding our Boston Whaler to the dock and jumped into the boat. Chris steered away, back along the shoreline of Westclaw Point toward the entrance to Busman's Harbor. Wyatt and Mom sat in the back, talking energetically. I was sure their conversation was about Windsholme, and I was deeply curious, but I couldn't hear them over the noise of the engine and the rush of the sea air.

Several times, Wyatt pulled out her cell phone, tapped on the keys, and stared at the sky, as if a satellite for the signal to bounce off would suddenly appear. Chris brought us through the mouth of the outer harbor, which was just wide and deep enough for the fishing trawlers and small cruise ships that sailed through it. We passed Dinkum's Light, a white lighthouse on a tiny island, where dozens of seals lay basking in the late afternoon sun. As the Victorian homes that lined Chipmunk Island came into view, I heard a distinctive *ding* that could only mean that Wyatt's cell was back online. My own phone vibrated in my pocket, downloading dozens of e-mail messages, stacked up after three days on Morrow Island.

Wyatt jumped from her seat in the stern, making her way to Chris and me. "Geoffrey says great for dinner. On his boat, the *Garbo,* at eight PM." She took off the big sunglasses and shaded her eyes with her hand. "There she is now."

As we came around Chipmunk Island, Wyatt pointed toward Blount's Hotel. Or at least toward the spot where it should have been. The old hotel was almost entirely obscured by the gigantic white boat. Yacht? It looked more like a battleship.

"She's a beauty," Chris said.

"Yup." Wyatt shielded her eyes and squinted into the late afternoon sun. "She's in town for a complete refit at Herndon Yachts, stem to stern. I designed the new interiors. I can't wait for you to see her. If you see the 'before,' you'll have a better appreciation for the 'after.'"

On the pier, we exchanged cell numbers—"just in case"—and went our separate ways.

* * *

At the apartment, Chris grabbed a shower first, his loud, off-tempo baritone echoing around the bathroom tiles. During the off-season, we'd run a dinner restaurant in Gus's space downstairs, where he served the best breakfasts and lunches in the harbor. Chris and I had never said we were officially living together, but most nights after working in the restaurant, we'd fallen into my bed upstairs, exhausted. Lots of his stuff had slowly migrated from his cabin to the apartment.

I'd never been in a serious relationship, and I'd expected working and living together to be claustrophobic, but it hadn't been. With a few small hiccups, Chris and I had fitted together like a well-oiled machine. The long winter had carried us from our first, tentative movements toward romance to "I love you," and then on to comfortable conversations that sailed seamlessly through talk about "next summer," "next Christmas," and "next year."

But when spring came, without really discussing it, we reverted to our old lives, almost as if the winter hadn't happened. I often stayed out on Morrow Island, and Chris frequently slept on his wooden sailboat, the *Dark Lady*, as he always had during tourist seasons in the past. It made no sense for him to stay on the island given how busy his spring was, as he rushed to open summer cottages, a service of his landscaping business. I'd been lucky to borrow him for a single day of work on the island, and I suspected it was only the lure of a conversation with an architect about restoring Windsholme that got him to give up the day's much-needed income.

Chris emerged from the bathroom and rooted in the closet that occupied one dormer of the studio apartment. "What do you wear to dinner on a yacht?" he called. His stuff was spread over three different locations, his cabin, his boat, and the studio, just as mine was spread out between my mom's house, the island, and the apartment. I longed for a place for both of us that was truly home.

"Clothes," I said, unhelpfully.

Chris ignored my sarcasm. "What's with you and Wyatt?" he called as he toweled himself off.

"Like I said, we went to boarding school together."

"Julia . . ." He let my name hang in the air. A warning.

"She was my first roommate freshman year."

"And?"

"And stuff. High school stuff. Not worth revisiting."

He pulled on a pair of khakis. "Honey, it's obvious there's something more between you two than a high school rivalry over the debate team. It's almost like you don't trust her."

I waited until he stood up straight so I could look him in the eye. "It didn't work out. It often doesn't with roommates. That's all."

"Didn't work out how?"

"Didn't work out the way those things don't work." I tried to keep the defensiveness out of my voice, but didn't succeed. I let out a long breath. "It's embarrassing."

"You can tell me. I was a teenager once too, you know."

"Yeah. Captain of the football team. Hell-raiser. You were a god." Our lockers had been next to each other when he was a senior and I was in eighth grade. Whenever he'd casually asked how I was doing, my knees had turned to jelly. I was always afraid I'd end up falling to the floor.

"You only think that because you were younger than me. I had my own stuff." He sounded a little hurt.

"She had some friends. They were kind of the Mean Girls." I looked around the tiny apartment, desperate not to go on. "I need to get in the shower." I hurried into the bathroom and closed the door.

As I stepped under the spray, I tried to focus on the cascading warm water and push Wyatt Jayne from my mind, but I didn't succeed.

I'd met Wyatt, then called Susan, the day I moved into my dorm at prep school in New Hampshire. Right after Mom and Dad said their good-byes, three girls arrived in the room. Wyatt introduced us. "This is my friend Amber from day school in Rye. And this is Melissa and Lainey. They went to a school just like ours only on the North Shore outside Chicago. They're the Amber and me of Winnetka! Julia lives on an island," she told them.

"Shouldn't you be at the foreign students' orientation?" Lainey asked. "It's going on right now in the chapel." Later, I would figure out that despite her polish and confidence, Lainey wasn't very bright.

"An island in the United States, off the coast of Maine," I clarified. "I only live there in the summer. Off-season we live in town."

"What town is that?" Amber asked, picking a lipstick off the bureau and whisking it across her lips with a practiced movement of the wrist I instantly envied.

"Wait till you hear this," Wyatt responded.

"Busman's Harbor," I answered.

"Her father's a lobsterman," Wyatt informed them.

"Grandfather," I corrected unnecessarily. It's not like my dad never worked his father's traps.

Melissa brightened. "My friend Cokie Henderson's family has a place there. Do you know her?'

Cokie. With a name like that, definitely a summer person. "No," I said.

"Oh." They quickly lost interest in me and engaged in a long conversation full of gossip about people I didn't know, discovering more and more connections between them, and leaving me more and more on the outside. I was used to not fitting in. In Busman's Harbor it had been because my mother was a former summer person, descendent of a once-wealthy family that owned a private island. In prep school it would be because my father's father was a lobsterman. *Great.*

"You keeping track of the time?" Chris called from outside the bathroom door.

"Coming!" I wrapped myself in a towel and

rummaged through my clothes rack. "This had better be an informal evening," I said. "Or else we're screwed."

Chris had added a white cotton dress shirt over the khakis. I went with a T-shirt dress that evoked an extra, extra long T-shirt more than a dress, but at least I'd made an effort. I slipped into my familiar black flats, my go-to whenever boots or sneakers wouldn't do.

"Should we take wine?" Chris asked.

I didn't want to show up empty-handed, but I couldn't imagine what wine we could bring to someone who owned a yacht that size. We went with two bottles, one red and one white, left over from our days of running our winter restaurant. I imagined the yacht's chef, or its sommelier—yacht sommelier, was that a thing?—quietly dumping the contents over the side.

We were headed toward the door when there was a sharp knock. Chris opened it and Quentin stood there. "You ready?"

I was relieved to see Quentin was in his usual blue shirt, khakis, and boat shoes and was holding a bouquet of peonies from his garden. That meant we weren't seriously underdressed. Or at least, if we were, we wouldn't be the only ones. I looked past Quentin at his gleaming, wood-sided estate wagon sitting in Gus's parking lot. That Quentin lived way out at the end of Westclaw Point, yet relied entirely on an antique car to get around, was one of his charming and mostly harmless eccentricities.

We walked over the harbor hill, past my mom's house, and crossed the footbridge that bisected the inner harbor. Quentin and Chris lingered on the bridge, staring at the gigantic yacht in front of Blount's.

"You guys can't fool me. You couldn't care less about this dinner party. You want to get on board that boat," I teased.

Chris smiled. "You got me."

Quentin was more circumspect. "I admit I've been staring at the *Garbo* for days, hoping for an invitation. But I'm also dying to meet Wyatt's mysterious boyfriend."

I realized I hadn't asked a thing about him. Not even our host's name. "Who is he?"

"Geoffrey Bower," Quentin answered with a breeziness I suspected was feigned. "You've heard of him, surely."

"I haven't," I said. "And don't call me Shirley."

"Bower was one of a handful of people who made a killing when the U.S. housing market collapsed," Quentin informed us.

"You mean like those guys in that book?" I asked. "And that movie?"

"Exactly. But he wasn't in either one. He never allowed it." Quentin paused for a minute to let a family of tourists pass. "Bower was reclusive even before he made his real fortune. He had a hedge fund and a hundred or so people whose money he invested. He never interacted with them except via e-mail. His lawyer and business partner, a man by the name of Seebold Frederickson, handled all the investor relations, did all the client schmoozing. They've been friends since boyhood. From what little I've gotten from people who knew them, Frederickson always ran interference between Geoffrey and the rest of the humans."

"And by 'made a killing' you mean . . . ?" Chris asked.

Quentin pointed to the mega-yacht tied up at Blount's. "Billions."

We were two weeks away from the longest day of the year, and even at that hour, the lines of the *Garbo* were clear from the footbridge. Chris leaned his arms on the railing. "How big do you think she is?"

Quentin stopped to admire her too. "Three hundred feet or so."

Chris whistled. "As long as a football field. That's insane." The *Garbo* was obviously old. An untraditional yacht, she looked almost military, like Geoffrey Bower was a small country.

"She's beautiful," Quentin said.

"Jealous?" I asked.

He grinned. "A little."

"So even the one percent has their one percent," Chris said.

Quentin laughed. "Yup. Whatever you have, someone else has a bigger one."

"C'mon, you guys," I urged. "We're going to be late. When we get there, you can see her up close." They fell into step on either side of me as we climbed the hill on the other side of the footbridge. "You said Bower was reclusive *even before* he made his fortune. What happened afterward?"

Quentin squinted in the gathering dusk. "After the housing market collapsed, the stock market collapsed—"

"You don't have to remind me." We'd almost lost our business because of a terrible loan my brother-in-law had persuaded my mother to take out during the go-go days before the crash.

"After the dust settled, Bower disappeared," Quentin finished.

"You mean like, *disappeared* disappeared. Like *poof*?" Chris used his hands to mime a small explosion.

"No. It was more orderly than that. He still invests money for a handful of his original clients."

"And nobody's seen him since the crash?" Chris asked. We were almost in front of Blount's Hotel and Marina.

"Wyatt has, obviously. And the staff on the yacht. But he hasn't appeared in public since." Quentin paused. "There's a Web site that tracks the movement of every registered yacht around the world. Spotters report when they see a boat in a port. Following Bower's movements has become a bit of a game for some people. There have been some fuzzy photos taken with long lenses, but he never leaves the *Garbo*. Ever. Periodically rumors run through the investment community that he's a drug addict, or has a beard down to his knees, or even is dead."

"And he's Wyatt's boyfriend? How does that work?" I wondered.

Quentin kept walking. "I can't wait to find out."

"No wonder you wanted to come so badly." My curiosity was piqued as well.

"Well, I hope he's alive," Chris said. "'Cause I'm hungry."

Chapter 3

A few minutes later, we arrived at Blount's Hotel. For the most part, pleasure boating in Maine was like an informal party. Tying up next to new people and chatting about where they'd been and where they were headed was part of the fun. The marina at Blount's was a different sort of place. For one thing, it had the only dockside moorings that could accommodate truly big yachts. And for another, you had to pass through the hotel and out its back door to access the boats. Blount's was a place for yachters who wanted privacy—celebrities, CEOs, heirs, and other assorted billionaires.

As we crossed the lobby, I stood straight, kept my eyes forward, and tried to look like I belonged. *Just here for a little dinner on one of the yachts. Nothing to see.* I recognized the kid behind the reception desk. His parents were friends of my mom's, and my sister had babysat for him when she was in high school. He waved and smiled as we walked by.

Exiting out the back door of Blount's, we took the

steep wooden steps down to the floating dock. The tide was low and the *Garbo* towered above us. Truth was, she would have done so at any tide. Up close, she looked even more like a warship, though the glimpses we had of the fittings spoke of luxury, not battle.

"Permission to come aboard!" Quentin shouted.

Wyatt's head hung over the deck above us, her sleek brown hair falling around her face. "You're here! Be right down."

Before Wyatt could reach us, a tall, tanned young man with tousled blond hair arrived. "G'day!" He carefully lowered the gangway. "Welcome aboard." When we reached the deck, Wyatt came up behind him, beaming.

We paused to put our shoes in the box provided, a yachting custom. No matter how formal the occasion, we would navigate it unshod. Even Chris and Quentin shed their boat shoes. Wyatt was barefoot too. Only the crew would wear footwear specifically approved for the ship's decking. My worn flats looked sad in the basket. They must have been the cheapest, oldest shoes ever left there. The blond man wordlessly took the crumpled brown bag with the wine bottles and the flowers from Quentin and disappeared.

Wyatt stood in front of a gleaming white wall, with the ship's logo, four slash marks of different sizes, and it's name painted in aqua. "I'm so glad you've come. Geoffrey is finishing up some work. Let me give you a tour while he's occupied."

Quentin stared at the logo for a moment. "Clever."

Wyatt smiled. "Thank you. I designed it. It was painted yesterday. A little experiment before the refit so we could see if it worked."

The logo didn't seem like anything to brag about until I took a second look. The slashes formed themselves into the cloche hat, eyebrow, nose, and mysterious smile of a glamorous woman. Greta Garbo, the ship's namesake, I assumed. Okay, so maybe it was clever.

Another man appeared behind Wyatt. He wasn't dressed in a uniform, but in dark slacks, a cream turtleneck, and a brown sports jacket that strained across his broad shoulders. For one confusing moment, I thought he might be Geoffrey, but then he grabbed a small basket off a side table, held it in front of him, and said, "Cell phones, please," in an accent I couldn't place.

I looked at Quentin, who shrugged and put his smartphone in the basket. Chris did the same. I hadn't brought the Snowden Family Clambake tote bag that usually went everywhere with me, so I didn't have a phone to contribute.

The man glanced in the basket. "These will be returned to you when you leave."

"Thank you, Emil," Wyatt said to his retreating back. "We'll start our tour with the staterooms since they're on this level. Remember, as I said, you're seeing the 'before.' I've designed the new interiors, with help from the experts at Herndon's. I've never done this sort of thing before. I'll show you the drawings when we get to Geoffrey's office. It's one deck up."

Herndon Yachts, with offices in Busman's Harbor and Monaco, was famous the world over for building new yachts, both sailing and motor, and refitting old ones. The age of transportation by ship might seem long ago to most people, but in Maine shipbuilding remained an important source of work. Bath Iron Works, just down the coast, was one of the largest employers in the state, making huge warships for the US Navy. The most modern ones, designed to evade radar and satellite photographs, looked like someone had forgotten to take off their gray paper wrapping.

At the other end of the spectrum was my friend Bud Barbour's boatyard, where he did minor repairs on local lobster boats. Maine offered those businesses and everything in between, including a place in Brooklin, where people From Away could pay to learn to build wooden boats in the manner of their ancestors. Or at least, in the manner of my ancestors.

Herndon's was an important source of local pride and well-paying jobs for people using new skills, like fabricating carbon-fiber hulls, and old skills, like cabinet and sail making. A complete refit at Herndon's meant that Wyatt would be visiting Busman's Harbor for many months, giving her plenty of time to persuade my mother to rebuild Windsholme. Still, I was happy the *Garbo* was in town. Keeping Herndon's pipeline full of new yacht orders and refits benefited all of us.

"This deck is the first living floor on the *Garbo*," Wyatt said. "So we'll start here. Below is the engine,

mechanicals, galley, crew quarters, a complete fitness
center. That sort of thing."

Quentin and Chris exchanged glances. I was sure
they'd have loved to see the engine room and other
inner workings, but they followed Wyatt as directed.
We passed through a set of double doors and she led
the way down a broad hallway carpeted at intervals
with oriental rugs that felt heavenly on my bare feet.
Quentin stooped to examine one, fingering its fibers
and smiling with admiration. The wood-paneled
walls and ceilings, teak floors, and elaborate mold-
ings made it hard to reconcile the inside of the
Garbo with its formidable outside. The hallway was
like one in a sumptuous country house. Slightly old
and slightly shabby, but still the ultimate in luxury.

Wyatt opened the door to the farthest stateroom
and we stepped inside.

Chris let out a low whistle. The room was enormous, dominated by a king-sized bed. Over its head-
board was a dazzling piece of art, a painting with
bold shapes that reminded me of pieces from the
1930s I'd seen in museums. The rest of the cabin
included a desk under the big windows that framed
views of Busman's Harbor, and a sitting area with a
flat screen TV that stuck out in the room like a sore
thumb.

"Let's see the head." Wyatt led us forward into
the bathroom. Hardly the usual cramped and basic
ship's facility, it was bigger than my room at Mom's
house and dripping with luxurious fixtures, an enormous tub, two pedestal sinks with round mirrors
above them.

"Holy moly." The words flew out of me before I could stop them.

"You see my challenge," Wyatt said.

"Updating the 1940s decor without losing its essence," Quentin supplied.

"Exactly."

When Quentin and Wyatt left the room, I reached for Chris's hand and held him back. "What was the deal with the guy who took the cell phones?" I whispered.

"Bodyguard," he whispered back. "He didn't want us to be able to take photos. Did you notice the bulge in his jacket?"

"Wow."

"Wow for sure. This is not your father's lobster boat."

We hurried to catch up to the others. Wyatt led us down the hall, opening one door after another to staterooms of equal size, each decorated like the others, with a hotel-like sameness. A five-star hotel to be sure, but a hotel nonetheless.

"The *Garbo* sleeps twenty guests," Wyatt said.

"Or five hundred refugees," Chris muttered.

"What? I didn't catch that." She most certainly had.

"Nothing," Chris answered. But I could tell it wasn't nothing to him.

We climbed a broad staircase, not at all shiplike, to the next deck. "The *Garbo* was originally built by the Canadian Navy," Wyatt said, in a tour-group-leader singsong. That explained the battleship lines. "When she was retired after World War Two, she was bought by a Greek billionaire. He spent millions transforming her into a luxury yacht, all in the hopes of seducing the film star Greta Garbo."

"Did it work?" Quentin asked.

Wyatt laughed. "Tragically, no. She spent a few nights aboard and never returned. But we use her name to this day."

I noticed the proprietary "we." I had assumed *Garbo* was a reference to Geoffrey Bower's reclusiveness, but the name predated his ownership.

On the next deck, Wyatt knocked on a set of doors with matching windows of Art Deco glass. It was the only entrance on that level. "Geoffrey?" There was no answer. "Oh, good, he's not here. Let's go in." We entered a stateroom that took up the entire level. "Geoffrey's cabin," she said.

An enormous bed stood in the center, something bigger than a California king. An Alaska king, perhaps? Off one side of the room was a bathroom twice the size of the one we'd already seen, a huge walk-in closet, and a small area with exercise equipment.

Wyatt noticed me looking at it. "There's a full gym belowdecks. Geoffrey lets the crew use it. He likes his privacy."

An office took up the entire other side of the space. It had built-in desks, with a half-dozen monitors on top of them, displaying talking heads with brightly colored bands of numbers running underneath them. Between the desks was a rectangular safe as tall as a man. It looked heavy and as old as the ship itself, except for the gleaming keypad that at some point must have replaced its original combination lock.

"Here are the drawings for the refit." Wyatt led us to the other end of the office where posterboard-backed, computer-generated color images sat on an easel. She flipped through them, showing us the cabins, Geoffrey's stateroom, the public rooms. I could see why Quentin had recommended her for Windsholme. Each of the designs felt fresh, yet still honored the *Garbo*'s heritage in the glamour of the 1940s. Despite my misgivings about Wyatt as a person, I was impressed.

"They're beautiful," I said.

"Yes," Chris agreed. "Perfect."

Quentin held out a hand and Wyatt passed him a drawing of the redone dining room. "Gorgeous."

"Thank you. That means so much." A blush spread from Wyatt's chest, up her delicate throat, and overtook her cheeks. Why did she care so much what Quentin thought?

Chapter 4

We finished the tour on the top deck by the swimming pool, its bottom lined with mosaic tiles that formed a portrait of Greta Garbo, a tribute to another man's obsession. I could see that the likeness, illuminated by the pool lights, had inspired Wyatt's logo. A yacht employee we'd not yet met stood behind the teak bar. "We'll take our cocktails here," Wyatt told him. She turned to us. "This is Rick, our head steward. He'll fix you whatever you'd like."

Quentin and Chris both seemed to take that as a challenge, asking for obscure top shelf whiskeys that Rick produced without so much as a search through the bottles displayed on the back bar, all the while bantering with them about quality of the liquor. He appeared to be in his forties, as deeply tanned as the other deckhand had been. He had dark hair on his head, worn short, and facial hair that might have been described as a small beard or a large goatee. He wore white pants and an aqua V-neck sweater, cashmere unless I was mistaken, with the ship's name over his right breast. His flawless English was delivered with a charming French accent that made me doubt his name was actually Rick. An Anglicism to help out the muddled Americans?

When the moment came, I asked for champagne. Wyatt said, "I'll join you." Rick opened a bottle and poured. We took our glasses to the heavily cushioned chairs on the deck, which were perfectly arranged for conversation. The sun had set and the sky behind the harbor hill still glowed a rich purple. The lights came on in the houses. I found the windows of my mother's yellow mansard Victorian, all lit up, always my beacon home.

I shivered in the fading light. June in Maine is not so warm. Wyatt noticed and asked Rick to bring me a sweater. An aqua cashmere cardigan appeared, also sporting the ship's name. I shrugged into it.

The glass door from the salon opened and a man walked onto the deck. "Ah, good evening," he said. "Wyatt's friends."

I didn't know what I had expected. I'd had so many contradictory impressions of Geoffrey before I met him. When Wyatt called him her boyfriend, I'd expected someone as turned-out, type A, and sophisticated as she was. When Quentin had described a reclusive financial genius, I thought of someone with a long beard and no social skills. Then, as Wyatt had walked us through the sleek yacht, I'd grown even more confused. What kind of a recluse needs a ship that sleeps twenty?

Where my imagination had ended up was nowhere close to the man who stood on the *Garbo*'s pool deck.

He was also older than I'd expected, midfifties, I guessed, two and a half decades older than Wyatt. He was short, pudgy, and pale, and wore white slacks, a blazer with gold buttons in it, and a jaunty yachtsman's cap. He was a caricature of a yacht owner, a Thurston Howell III. And, unless I was very much mistaken, he was wearing a brown wig under the cap.

He strode over to where we stood, grabbed Quentin's hand, and pumped enthusiastically. "You must be Tupper. Wyatt has told me so much about you." Quentin opened his mouth to return the greeting, but Geoffrey had already turned to me. "And you're Julia, the old school friend."

Friend? Not exactly. But I admitted I was Julia and allowed my arm to be moved up and down.

Geoffrey kept going. "And you are?" He was clearly puzzled by Chris.

"Chris Durand, Julia's boyfriend." Chris took Geoffrey's proffered hand.

"Welcome aboard." Geoffrey looked around our little group and clapped his hands together. "I apologize for the delay. Some urgent business I had to take care of. Let's eat, shall we?"

The dining room table could have easily sat thirty, but just one end of it had been set. Rick, the goateed steward, held out the chair to the right of the head and gestured for me to take a seat. He did the same for Wyatt on the left. The men took their seats, Geoffrey at the head and Quentin and Chris on the outside.

The chairs were heavy, the table fixed to the

deck. The room had the feel of an elegant, and very expensive, restaurant. The china was restaurant grade, heavier than what you'd have in a home, better for a yacht that would be moving. The silver was also heavy, probably sterling, with a wave pattern on the handles; the water goblets were lead crystal.

Rick glided up to the table with a bottle of wine wrapped in a cloth napkin. Geoffrey gestured for Wyatt to taste it. She nodded her approval and the glasses were filled with the pale liquid. We chatted about the things strangers chat about. Weather, sports, places to explore along the Maine coast. Geoffrey nixed some of the obvious ports, Bar Harbor and Camden. "Too many people." He talked excitely of the refit at Herndon's.

"Where will you stay while the work is done?" I asked.

Wyatt cut in. "Geoffrey has chartered another yacht. Something a little smaller."

Rick returned through the dining room's service entrance with the first course. Raw oysters served on beautiful china oyster plates decorated in the *Garbo*'s colors, along with personal-sized servings of Tabasco, horseradish, and cocktail sauce. I reached for the small oyster fork to the right of my spoons. The only fork ever placed to the right, my mother had taught Livvie and me. Quentin's mother had evidently done the same, or maybe he'd hired a fork tutor when he made his first million. Chris, however, grabbed the most prominent fork on the left, his dinner fork, and dug in. The delicious shellfish were undoubtedly from the Damariscotta River, just one peninsula up and famous for its oyster farms.

As we ate, Geoffrey turned to me. "Tell me about my dear Wyatt when you girls were at school." His blue-gray eyes opened wide in anticipation.

I stared back. I had no warm and fuzzy anecdotes about the teenaged Wyatt to offer. "She was the captain of the debate team," I stammered.

"I don't doubt it. She and I had many a debate when we were choosing the appointments for the refit." He'd removed the silly yachtsman's cap and I had trouble not staring at the wig. Why would a man who could buy anything wear something that was so fake looking? But then, getting hair plugs or having a quality toupee made would require going ashore. Or allowing other humans on board. Or maybe he saw so few people, his looks didn't matter. Which brought me back to my original thought about the wig: Why wear it?

But, confusingly, I saw no sign of antisocial behavior from Geoffrey. Quite the opposite. He chatted easily with everyone as Wyatt hovered near him proprietarily, touching his arm and fidgeting whenever he engaged with someone else too long. She used the same tired, flirty behaviors she'd tried on Quentin and Chris—the batting eyelashes, the whisper in the ear. It seemed almost like she was trying to win Geoffrey over, not like there was an established relationship.

Rick cleared the oyster plates and served the salads American-style, before the main course. Without drawing attention, he replaced Chris's fork. Flawless service. If the oysters had been in the riverbed that morning, the greens and the raw, fresh peas in the simple salad had been picked at the same time. There was something familiar about the flavor of the dressing. It dredged up a memory, but the more I chased it, the fuzzier it got.

Quentin put down his salad fork (Chris had persisted with his dinner fork strategy) and looked at Geoffrey, finally asking what I knew he'd been dying to all along. "I'm not going to ask how you knew the housing market would collapse. I want to know how you had the certainty to place such a huge bet. It was your entire fortune, wasn't it? And money you invested for your clients. That took guts. I'm not sure, even if I'd seen the crash coming, I would have had the nerve."

"Ah," Geoffrey answered. "Without risk, life isn't interesting, is it?"

Quentin did ask him some technical questions and they chatted in low voices a few minutes, but perhaps eager not to talk about it, or perhaps, like a good host, sensing Chris's attention drifting off, Geoffrey turned the conversation back to the *Garbo*.

The men discussed her length, speed, engine size, even the capacity of her hot water heater. I let the conversation wash over me, marveling, not for the first time, at the capacity of men to turn any interesting conversation into a long string of numbers.

Rick served the next course, which he announced as Tarragon Ricotta Gnocchi with Lobster Velouté. I took a bite, prepared for a dish too rich to enjoy, but the gnocchi was light, the taste of the lobster in the sauce definite, but delicate. Like the salad dressing, the velouté tasted familiar and I strained to remember when I'd eaten a similar dish. It was all so good, so perfectly cooked.

Rick cleared the small plates and reappeared with the main course. I thought I was too full, but the piece of cod, flavored with lemon and herbs, and the tiny asparagus seduced me.

The steward brought coffee and dessert, small dishes of strawberry granita. We all complimented the meal. Geoffrey looked gratified. "Rick, ask the chef to come up to receive our appreciation," he instructed.

Rick nodded and disappeared. A few minutes later the service door opened and a young woman entered, wearing a double-breasted chef's coat sporting the *Garbo* name, and a white toque covering her dark hair.

I jumped out of my seat and ran to embrace her. "Genevieve! What are you doing here?"

Chapter 5

The members of the *Garbo*'s crew sat crowded around the tiny table in their dining area, eating the same gnocchi course we guests had finished, though in larger servings. With Geoffrey's permission, Genevieve had invited Chris, Quentin, and me to visit the galley. Wyatt had declined to come along: "I've seen it."

Once we were down there, I was grateful. One more person would have made the tiny space impossible to maneuver. Getting to the galley required navigating a maze of steep stairways, appropriately called ladders on a ship, and narrow passages. I was impressed that Rick had moved the food from below to the service pantry, and then on into the dining room, so smoothly. On the *Garbo*, it was still a world of upstairs, downstairs.

Genevieve introduced the people at the table. Emil, the security guy, and Rick, the head steward, we'd already met. The tousled-haired mate who'd helped us aboard was an Australian named Ian. The others were Marius, the captain; Doug, the engineer; and Maria Consuelo, the junior stewardess. They stood in turn and shook our hands. Aside from Genevieve, Doug was the only American, not at all unusual for a yacht crew.

Doug sized up Chris and Quentin quickly. "Would you gentlemen like to see the big-boy toys and leave the ladies to visit?" He was a bantam rooster of a man, his dark hair slicked back, his skin pale, perhaps because his work was in the bowels of the ship, not on deck. He stood straight, with his chest puffed out.

Quentin and Chris nodded enthusiastically and left for a tour of the engine room and other internal workings of the yacht. The rest of the crew slowly cleared out of the dining area, stopping to clean off their dishes and stack them neatly in the galley sink before they went.

Genevieve fixed herself a plate of gnocchi and sat down at the table, motioning for me to sit next to her. It was after ten o'clock, but she wouldn't eat until dinner service, both for the owner and the crew, was complete. No wonder the salad dressing and velouté tasted familiar. I'd eaten them before, prepared by Genevieve.

"Spill," I commanded. "What are you doing here?"

Genevieve swallowed her food and blotted her lips with a cloth napkin. "After I closed my restaurant in Portland, I was lost for a while."

Though only twenty-six, Genevieve had been a wunderkind seafood chef and part owner of a small chain of five seaside restaurants spread along the Maine coast. But she'd chosen the wrong business partner, and after he was murdered and no longer able to prop up the restaurants with constant infusions of cash, the business had collapsed. Genevieve had fought to hold on to her flagship Portland restaurant in that city's competitive foodie scene, but during a snowy February, she explained, even that goal had become impossible.

I had met Genevieve when her business partner was murdered, strung up under my brother-in-law Sonny's dad's lobster boat in Busman's Harbor. I'd tried, at the time, to throw her under the bus with the state police detectives investigating the case, if only to move their suspicions away from Sonny. It hadn't worked, for a number of reasons, chief among them being she wasn't guilty. And, as I found out later, because the detective sergeant on the case was falling in love with her.

"I'm sorry about your restaurant," I said.

"Don't be," she said. "In some ways, I felt like I'd been liberated. I've had responsibilities for running kitchens since I was fifteen. A friend in the business told me about this amazing opportunity. I could spend the rest of the winter sailing around the Mediterranean on a mega-yacht cooking for the crew and a single man who never entertained. I'd often toyed with the idea of being a private chef and the promise of sunlight, travel. . . . I couldn't resist. I flew to Sardinia, where I had a quick interview with Mr. Bower and was hired on the spot. I'd brought next to nothing with me. I had to buy clothes in every port. Luckily, I was wearing my chef's whites most of the time."

"Was it wonderful?" I'd spent my winter, an unusually harsh one, in Maine for the first time in sixteen years, and the idea of a yacht on the Côte d'Azur seemed like a dream.

Genevieve smiled. "It was. From Sardinia we sailed to Corsica, then Monte Carlo, Antibes, and Saint-Tropez. It was early, before the season began, so the ports weren't crowded and it was chilly, but every stop was beautiful. Mr. Bower instructed me to buy local ingredients wherever we went. Cooking in a galley was an adjustment"—she gestured around the tiny space—"and cooking when the boat was underway was an adventure, but honestly, I loved it."

"Tom couldn't have been happy." Sergeant Tom Flynn had been one of the investigators in Genevieve's partner's murder, though they hadn't become a couple until after it was solved. He'd rearranged his life for her, moving to Portland as she tried to save her restaurant, and applying for a transfer so he could stay with her.

"He wasn't, though he worked hard to hide it. The saving grace was knowing I'd be back in Maine this spring. Mr. Bower plans to stay in the area with a skeleton crew while the *Garbo* is refit. We'll do a little cruising on the yacht he's chartered, but we won't leave the area until the fall. Tom's coming up tomorrow morning. We're staying at the Snuggles. You'll have to come over and say hello."

The Snuggles Inn was a bed-and-breakfast across the street from Mom's house, run by the Snugg sisters, who were old family friends and honorary great aunts. I wasn't sure Sergeant Flynn would want to devote any of his time with Genevieve to me. I'd been involved in a few of his homicide cases during the previous year, and he'd never been a fan of mine. Then we'd worked together on one case over Christmas while his boss was on vacation, and though that had gone a little better, I still wouldn't have called us friends.

"What's the crew like?" I asked.

"Like a family. We're from every corner of the earth, but we work hard and have each other's backs."

She showed me around the galley, pointing out the gimbals on the marine stove's legs, designed to keep it level as the ship moved, and the guards around the stovetop to keep pots from sloshing about. The *sous-vide* device she'd used to cook the cod still sat in its pot of water. I couldn't imagine Genevieve putting out the haute cuisine meal we'd just consumed from the tiny space and told her so. "I never could have cooked the fish like that if we were underway," she said.

"I don't see how you do it."

She laughed. "Are you kidding? I have it easy. Most yachts are loaded with guests all the time and many are rented out as charters. More guests mean more parties and bigger crews. The *Garbo* has been a great place to learn and figure out what works, but honestly I wish it were livelier. Maybe it will be soon."

"Why would it change?" I asked.

She ducked her head. "I was referring to Ms. Jayne. Maybe if her relationship with Mr. Bower progresses? Don't say anything to her, but Geoffrey's asked everyone to stay off the boat tomorrow night and asked me to prepare a cold supper for two— caviar, shrimp, asparagus, a lobster salad and chocolate strawberries, all with a big red lobster body as the centerpiece. He has a romantic evening planned."

"How are your accommodations?" I asked.

"I share a tiny cabin with Maria Consuelo. She's—"

"Young," I supplied.

"Young, naive, inexperienced. This is her first job out of stew school. Rick hired her because he's softhearted. And he doesn't want to make beds and clean bathrooms, even though it's only Mr. Bower and, for the past week, Ms. Jayne."

"How long have Wyatt and Geoffrey been dating?" I couldn't contain my curiosity any longer.

"Several months," Genevieve answered. "But it's mostly been long distance. I look at it this way. I have no housing costs. I'm saving nearly every penny of my generous salary. I'd like to have my own restaurant again someday. Financed by me, not by some terrible partner."

"You'll do it, Genevieve. I'm sure you will."

But Genevieve wasn't listening to me. Her head was tilted up as footsteps, lots of pounding footsteps, ran across the deck above us. "Oh, drat," she said. "They're here."

Genevieve and I ran up the narrow stairways to the main deck.

"Who's here?" I panted. "What's happening?"

She didn't take time to answer.

The rest of the crew, along with Chris and Quentin, was already there, hanging over the side, ogling the spectacle below. Under the marina's lights a Blount's bellboy and the desk clerk, along with a man in a suit who had to be the hotel manager, were engaged in a shouting match with four people down on the dock.

"What the—" Chris said.

Each of the four people held a handmade sign. OCCUPY BLOUNT'S, one of them said. STOP THE 1 PERCENT, and PEOPLE NOT PROFITS, said the others. There were three male protesters, whose faces I couldn't make out. I did recognize the bent figure of Matilda Patterson, well-known local gadfly. Her sign, which was strung across the front of her walker, said, SCREW THE RICH. If the rumors were true, in her younger days, she had.

"We have the right to lawful assembly," the guy holding the OCCUPY BLOUNT'S sign shouted. He was taller than the other two men and stood slightly in front of the group. It seemed like he was the leader.

"Again, this is private property," the man in the suit said. "You must leave."

"You don't own the ocean, buddy," one of the younger men yelled.

"Again, I point out, you are not *in* the ocean." The manager was losing his patience. "You are standing on our dock, which is private property." He put his hand to his brow and squinted up at the gang of us on the *Garbo*, then turned back to the protesters. "Leave immediately, or I'll call the police."

The leader shrugged. "Go ahead."

Emil, the bodyguard, called down to the Blount's employees. "I'm disembarking."

But by the time Ian, the blond deckhand, had the gangway in place, the Blount's manager was already on his cell phone. If Emil could get off the *Garbo* via the gangway, didn't that mean the protesters could rush on? Though I had to admit, they didn't look particularly ferocious, especially compared to the broad-shouldered Emil, with his visible jacket bulge.

Two Busman's Harbor cops showed up about two minutes later, as speedy a response as I would have expected on a Thursday evening before the season was fully underway. There wasn't that much for them to do. My friend, Jamie Dawes, and his partner, Pete Howland, probably represented the entirety of our on-duty police force. Jamie moved down the long wooden steps to the dock with nimble confidence. Pete, of the round gut, took a little longer.

"What seems to be the problem?" Jamie flashed his perfect teeth, friendly and engaging, meant to bring the temperature on the dock down.

"We have guests on the yacht who are being obstructed from disembarking." Emil exaggerated. We hadn't said our good-byes and the protesters had so far not prevented us from doing anything. But we did have to get off the ship at some point.

Jamie looked up at the faces hanging over the rail and spotted me. "Figures," he said, loud enough for us all to hear. He turned to the protesters. "This dock is private property. The manager has asked you to leave. Move along and there won't be any problems." He and Howland stood on either side of the end of the gangway and spread their arms. "C'mon down," Jamie called.

I looked at Chris, who nodded slightly, a "let's get out of here" signal. I gave Genevieve a hug and murmured, "See you soon." I was at the top of the gangway before I remembered I was barefoot. "Wait, I—"

Rick appeared with our shoes and cell phones. We put them on. I remembered I was still wearing the *Garbo* sweater and hastily pulled it off.

Chris, Quentin, and I went down the gangway. Emil stood at the bottom, arms folded, glowering. "Tell Geoffrey and Wyatt thank you for the lovely dinner," I stammered. "I didn't even—"

He cut me off. "I am sure they understand."

We walked through the passageway created by the cops. Jamie barely suppressed his laughter. I made a face at him. The atmosphere, never as threatening as Emil had made it out to be, was by then practically jolly. It was hard to take Matilda and the sign on her walker seriously. I looked at the other three protesters as I went by. Up close, I recognized two of the men, local guys in their early twenties, probably more interested in beer than in Geoffrey Bower's alleged financial shenanigans. The tall man was definitely a stranger. He was older than I expected, early forties and incredibly handsome, with a swoop of rich brown hair that came over his forehead. He was dressed in khakis and a madras shirt, with a cotton sweater draped over his shoulders, preppy style. Hardly the wild-eyed anarchist.

Chris, Quentin, and I continued up the steps to Blount's big patio. I turned at the top to see the three male protesters midway up, with Matilda and her walker, assisted by Jamie, and trailed by Officer Howland, bringing up the rear. On the dock, Emil was having an emphatic and apparently unhappy conversation with the Blount's employees. I couldn't blame him. It must have taken a good bit of time for Matilda to get down to the dock in the first place, and the staff had all somehow missed her. It didn't say much for Blount's security. But then people, even very rich people, didn't expect to be bothered in our little corner of the universe.

Chapter 6

"You're awfully quiet." Chris reached for my hand as we walked up Main Street. It was almost eleven o'clock. Quentin had hurried on ahead to pick up his car. After he retrieved it, he still had to make the long drive out to his house at the end of Westclaw Point.

As Chris and I came up the steep harbor hill, I expected Mom's house to be dark. Instead it was lit up like a lantern—light glowing in every window. I walked a little faster, worried. What could this be about?

"I want to stop in at Mom's."

Chris nodded and picked up his pace to match my own. He'd noticed the lights too. The front door was, as always, unlocked, and as it swung open, I heard the unmistakable wails of a baby. "Mom!"

"In the kitchen."

Mom stood in the center of her big, old-fashioned kitchen, jiggling my distraught nephew in her arms. Jack was four months old and so far had distinguished himself as the most easygoing baby any of us had ever met.

"What's wrong?"

"Teething." Mom used her free hand to take a teething ring out of the freezer and apply it to Jack's gums.

"Can we help?" I'd no sooner got the words out when there was a *whoop*, a *boom*, and a *crash* from upstairs. "What the heck?"

"Page," Mom answered. "She has a friend sleeping over, though there hasn't been any sleeping yet. Julia, can you go up and settle them? Chris, hold Jack. I'm going to fix him some milk and see if he'll drop off."

Mom handed Chris the baby as I made for the back stairs, and lo and behold, Jack's hysterical cries subsided to a gurgling whine. "Wow," Mom said to Chris. "I'm impressed."

I found Page and her friend running up and down the hallway on the second floor. They were both in pajamas and giggling wildly.

"Whoa, whoa. What's going on up here?" I used my sternest tone.

"Hi, Aunt Julia," Page gasped out between giggles.

"Hi, Aunt Julia," the friend mimicked.

"What's your name?" I asked.

The girl looked at me with saucer-sized eyes that took my breath away. The irises were rimmed in a deep green. I knew only one other person with eyes that color. Chris. The girl opened her mouth, but didn't seem to be able to answer me.

Those eyes momentarily stunned me. The unique color couldn't be a coincidence, could it?

"She's Vanessa!" Page shouted, bringing me back into the moment. "Vanessa-bessa, bo-bessa, banana, fanna, fo-fessa!" The two of them collapsed in a giggly heap. Vanessa had tawny brown hair, worn long and disheveled from the hijinks of the evening. She was tiny and thin. They made an odd pair. Page, with her wild red hair and broad swimmer's shoulders, had inherited her parents' height.

"Okay, okay, let's settle down here. It's way past bedtime and Grammy's got enough on her hands with Jack."

"He's a baby," Page observed, giggling hard. *Hilarious.*

"Into your room," I commanded. "And beds." I walked them back down the hall to the room my mother had decorated in pink and princesses for Page. When my dad had been dying six years earlier, my sister, Livvie, and a young Page spent so many nights at the house, Mom decided Page should have her own room.

Page climbed on her twin bed and Vanessa settled on a mattress on the floor. Le Roi, the Maine coon cat I'd adopted in the fall, came out from wherever he'd been hiding during the fracas, jumped onto Page's bed, purred, kneaded the quilt, and lay down beside her. He was thirty pounds of cat, a big boy even for a coon, and insisted on lying horizontally, practically pushing her off the bed. But she closed her eyes contentedly and gave him a rub.

Though he'd spent the winter in my apartment,

Le Roi was staying with Mom while I was shuttling back and forth to Morrow Island. When school ended on Monday, he'd move to the island with Livvie's family. He was more of a family cat than just my own. I'd miss him, but I couldn't deprive him of a life wild and free on the island, with clambake guests slipping him pieces of lobster under their tables.

"Tell us a story," Page begged.

I didn't want to leave Chris and Mom for too long, but a story might keep the girls in their beds. I looked at Vanessa's pale face and huge, deeply circled, green eyes. Page could go on for hours, but this girl needed to sleep and the next day was a school day.

"Give me a minute." I crept to the top of the back stairs and listened. Jack was quiet. Chris and Mom talked in low tones. I returned to Page's room. "Okay," I told the girls. "I'm back. One story."

"The Lady on the Stairs!" Page called out. "You'll love it," she assured Vanessa.

"Okay, okay. The Lady on the Stairs."

Like every town with old houses, lighthouses, ships, and a big body of water, Busman's Harbor offered lots of legends, complete with nightly ghost walks for tourists. At frequent intervals, paranormal "experts" arrived in town with funny instruments to check out different places. You couldn't run a self-respecting B&B without a ghost. Windsholme had two ghosts, and the story of the Lady on the Stairs was Page's favorite.

I turned out the overhead light, pulled my phone out of my pocket, turned on the flashlight app, and sat cross-legged at the end of Vanessa's mattress, shining the light on my face.

"These events happened in the olden days," I intoned, "but they echo down to us today."

"Oooh," Page said, knowing what was coming.

"It was at Windsholme, on Morrow Island. Have you ever been to Morrow Island?" I asked Vanessa.

"No," she answered in a soft, quivery voice.

"You'll have to visit this summer." I settled into my tale. "Lenora Bailey was a maid out there. She was only nineteen years old. The family loved her, especially the young Morrow boys, William and Charles." I had added this last little detail to the story only recently when I'd learned more about my family's history. "One day clouds gathered and the wind began to blow. The waves crashed on the rocks." I made crashing sounds, undulating my hands in front of the light from the phone.

"Go on, go on." Page was impatient, but Vanessa didn't make a sound.

"The servants waited for Lenora to come down, but she was late. Another maid went to her room on the top floor and returned saying Lenora was sick with terrible pains in her stomach. The family was alerted and arrangements were made to take her to the doctor in Busman's Harbor on the sailing yacht the family kept at the dock. But by the time the plans were made, the captain said it was too stormy to go, the ship would crash on the rocks, and he and Lenora and anyone else aboard would surely perish."

I waited, listening to the girls' rapid breathing. I wanted to tell a good story, but I didn't want to terrify them. Page had heard the tale dozens, maybe hundreds of times, but if Vanessa had nightmares, Mom would be the one who'd have to deal with it.

I continued. "The gardener, Randy Brownly, was in love with Lenora. He insisted he could go to town in a little skiff and bring back the doctor safely. Anything to save his true love." I had no idea if the gardener's name was Randy. I had no idea if any of it was true. I suspected my father had made up the story. Though the Morrows were Mom's ancestors, Dad was the storyteller, and after twenty-five years of running the Snowden Family Clambake, he'd had as much claim to Morrow Island as anyone.

"The family forbade it. They argued that even if Randy somehow made it to town, the doctor would never agree to come back with him over such a rough sea. By then it was pouring rain, in addition to the wind and the waves, and so dark it was like nighttime.

"But Randy didn't listen. He snuck off in the little boat when no one was looking. Meanwhile, Lenora got sicker and sicker. Her fever spiked and she fell in and out of consciousness, but in her lucid moments, she begged for her true love to come." I did Lenora's voice, young and weak with illness. "'Randy, where is my Randy?' At first, the other servants lied and told her he was outside securing the island for the storm. But finally, they had to tell her Randy had gone to fetch the doctor for her. They assured her he would be back soon, even though none of them believed it.

"The storm raged and night fell. Lenora got sicker

and sicker and there was no sign of Randy. Finally, Lenora died. Her last words were, 'Where are you, my Randy, my love? Why haven't you come to bid me good-bye?' All the servants and the family cried because they loved Lenora so.

"The next morning the sun rose bright. The sea was calm and the storm was gone. The townspeople in Busman's Harbor found the broken shards of Randy's little boat on the beach. Randy had never made it to town. His body was never found. Lenora's relations buried her in the town cemetery, but they say she roams the halls of Windsholme still, searching for her Randy. They say she'll never rest until she finds him."

I paused dramatically, and then intoned in rich, ringing tones, "Many visitors to Windsholme have seen her, standing on the landing that overlooks the great hall, dressed in her maid's uniform with a glowing white apron, gazing out to sea, crying for her Randy, the love of her life. The love of her death." I took a deep breath. "Do you see her? Do you hear her—calling, calling? BOO!"

Both girls rewarded me with loud squeals. Page exhaled rapidly. "Have you ever seen her, Aunt Julia? I never have. I wonder where she stands and waits now that you burned down the front staircase?"

"I didn't—"

"And isn't it funny," Page continued, "how Lenora's last name is Bailey, like yours, Vanessa?"

Silence. I couldn't see Vanessa in the darkened room, but I could imagine the saucer-like green eyes opened as wide as they could get. I was possibly the worst babysitter ever.

I got both girls settled and headed down the back stairs. Vanessa seemed exhausted. I didn't think the scare I'd given her would keep her up long.

Mom and Chris sat at the kitchen table talking quietly. Chris had a sleeping Jack cradled in his lap. Standing out on the back stairs, I went all broody and gooey on the inside. What hormone gets released at the sight of a man holding an infant, bringing on that surge of maternal longing? Particularly a man you love?

The thought brought me back to Vanessa's green eyes. There had been a lot of women in Chris's life before me, but no children that I knew about. And since, after a rocky start, we were honest with each other, none that he knew about, I thought, as well. I pushed the thought away. Mom's house was not the place to discuss it.

I caught my breath and continued down to the kitchen. "How did you end up with this houseful of kids, anyway?" I asked Mom.

"Livvie and Sonny went to a concert in Portland," she answered. "Their first date night since Jack was born, and likely their last until after tourist season. Vanessa's mom pulled a double shift at Crowley's. She was desperate, so Livvie offered my services. Livvie and Sonny are coming to pick up Jack when they get back to the peninsula, but we decided it was better for the girls to spend the night."

"Who's Vanessa's mom? You must know her," I said to Chris. One of his three jobs was working as a bouncer at Crowley's. So far this season, he'd only worked Saturday nights, but it would be more nights once the summer heated up.

"A little bit. She's a waitress over there, a single mom. Lives on Thistle Island with two kids."

It seemed like he barely knew her.

"I gather Vanessa and Page have become close friends at school," Mom said.

Mom asked a few questions about the *Garbo*, her eyes widening as we described its beautiful appointments, all due to be updated in the refit and the fancy meal. In glowing terms Chris described Wyatt's designs for the ship while I sat quietly. I couldn't deny the pictures had been gorgeous, but I didn't want to encourage my mother to go down that road.

A vehicle door slammed outside in the driveway, and then another. Livvie and Sonny walked through the front door.

"Wow," Livvie said, spotting the sleeping Jack. "The baby's asleep and no sound from the girls? Mom, you're a miracle worker."

"Piece of cake." Mom stood. "Wyatt Jayne is coming to give us her preliminary thoughts on rebuilding Windsholme at ten tomorrow. Who's coming? You're all invited."

"Work," Chris said.

"Traps," Sonny answered. Until the Snowden

Family Clambake opened, he was helping his dad pull lobster traps.

"Jack," Livvie answered, her all-purpose excuse for everything. "I'll pick up the girls for school tomorrow morning, but ten o'clock will be right in the middle of Jack's nap."

"I'll be here." There was no way I was leaving Mom alone with the persuasive skills of Wyatt Jayne.

We all walked out to the drive. Livvie and Sonny put Jack in his car seat and drove away. The long day hit me like a frying pan to the face. It had been filled with heavy lifting out in the sun and sea air, followed by wine, more wine, a huge meal, and more than a few surprises. I gave Mom a hug and promised to be back in time to meet with Wyatt in the morning.

On the walk back to the apartment, I thought about mentioning Vanessa's striking green eyes, but decided I was too tired to form a question, and Chris was too tired to give an answer. The most likely outcome was a testy conversation about nothing. Better to wait until another time.

Chapter 7

In the morning the smells from Gus's restaurant interrupted a dream where I was lost in the mazelike passages of a battleship while being chased by a creature with giant green eyes. I sat up in bed, shaking the images away, and listened to the buzz of indistinct conversation and the bang of iron skillets coming from downstairs. My stomach grumbled. I reached over and shook Chris. "Get up. Pancakes await."

By the time we were dressed and downstairs, Gus's was filled to capacity. Gus catered to the local crowd—exclusively. If he didn't know you, or you couldn't provide a local connection, you didn't eat. This time of year all his diners had places to go, people to see, jobs to get done. There'd be no lingering over second cups of coffee like in the off-season.

Chris and I were lucky to snag the last two seats at the counter. I swiveled on my stool to stare at the place our bar had occupied when we'd run our dinner restaurant at Gus's over the winter. At his insistence, when we returned to our summer jobs, the bar had been disassembled and stowed away. The single candlepin bowling lane that had occupied the space from time immemorial was back, though I had never seen a single person use it.

"What'll ya have?" Gus deposited two steaming mugs of coffee in front of us, mine with milk, Chris's black.

"Blueberry pancakes," I answered immediately. This time of year the tiny Maine low-bush berries would be frozen, but some blueberries were always better than no blueberries. Chris opted for eggs over easy, clam hash, home fries, and toast.

"I hear you were on that big yacht over at Blount's last night," Gus said. His great white eyebrows swept together over his nose like seagulls in flight.

You can't make a move without the whole town knowing. Normally, the comings and goings of people From Away held no interest for Gus, but a yacht the size of the *Garbo* created an exception.

"Yup." Chris didn't seem to share my qualms about privacy. "We had dinner and got a tour."

"How'd you get an invite like that?"

Chris spread his arms out as far as the crowded counter allowed. "Julia's school friend is the girl-friend of the owner."

"We weren't friends," I snapped, to Gus's retreating back. He poured pancake batter on the grill.

When Gus delivered our food, he lingered, crossing his arms in front of him and taking his pointy chin in his hand. "So how big an engine you reckon a boat like that has?"

Chris described the engine with enthusiasm while Gus nodded. Before long, the guys on either side of us were in the conversation. I drifted away, digging into my pancakes. Gus might not be light and fluffy, but his pancakes were and they made the world a better place.

"How much fuel does she carry?" my seatmate asked. "How much d'ya suppose it costs to fill her up?"

Chris had neglected to ask this question when he got his tour, so they all took turns speculating. I didn't tune back in until I heard Chris say, "She's an architect who's helping Jacqueline decide whether to rebuild Windsholme."

I gave Chris the stink eye. We'd carefully not discussed fixing up Windsholme around town, or the money that had fallen into my mother's lap to do it.

Chris knew instantly what I was protesting. "What? If you restore Windsholme, everyone in town is going to know about it sooner or later."

Gus observed us, taking it all in, but not saying a word. He turned back to his grill and cleaned it vigorously.

In the parking lot, Chris gave me a quick kiss on the lips. "I'm sleeping on the *Dark Lady* tonight," he said. "Have some work to do on her that will keep me there late. You staying on the island?"

"I guess so." The clambake had to be ready to open in six days.

"Great," he said with a smile. "See you."

* * *

I stood in front of Mom's house, unable to remember the walk over from Gus's. Chris's breezy "See you!" had taken up most of my mental space. On the one hand, there was no reason to look for trouble in our relationship. Chris loved me, plain and simple. Over the long winter, I'd grown to know him as a man who said what he thought, without filters or agendas. My eighth-grade crush on him had matured into love.

But that was Off-Season Chris. Tourist-Season Chris was a different matter. Last summer, he'd disappeared for days at a time, doing something that was perhaps morally defensible, but certainly illegal. He'd given it up on his own, before I'd discovered what he was doing. It had taken me a long time to get past it, but over the near–honeymoon-like off-season, I'd learned to trust again.

So there was no reason to obsess about the bit of distance that had crept into our relationship. It was spring; we were both overwhelmed with preparations for the tourist season. That explained it. There was nothing to worry about. Except there was Vanessa with her green, green eyes.

"Are you going to stand there like a statue all day?"

"Mom." I hadn't seen her come out onto the porch. "I need to work on a few things in the clambake office before Wyatt and Quentin get here."

Mom opened the screen door and waved me in.

"The girls are gone?" I asked as I passed through.

"Livvie picked them up for school."

I went to my father's office on the second floor.

It was still dominated by his big oak desk and looming metal file cabinets. For the past year, as I'd worked there, the old furniture had comforted me, as if Dad was looking over my shoulder and cheering me on. But now I wondered if it wasn't time to put my own stamp on the place, replace his old prints of ships being buffeted by gales with something more feminine and cheery. Could Mom handle it if I changed the decor? I didn't want her to feel I was erasing him.

I called our produce supplier to make sure our delivery of potatoes, onions, and corn was on track for the day before Family Day, a sort of dress rehearsal for the clambake we held every year for staff, family, and friends. The ears of corn were frozen and came from somewhere down south. New England wouldn't harvest any fresh corn for a couple of months, but like the other items, corn on the cob was a traditional part of the clambake. I called one of the guys who supplied us with the clams we used for steamers. He was upbeat, optimistic. Great season so far, he assured me. Our order would be filled.

The doorbell *ponged* and the sound of voices traveled up the front stairs.

"Julia! Quentin and Wyatt are here!"

Mom let them in as I came down the stairs. Wyatt was dressed in another dynamite shift, brown hair shiny. Her makeup was light but perfect, the kind of application that says, "I cared enough about this meeting to fix my face for you, but honestly, I'm so good-looking I don't really need it."

"Come sit in the kitchen," Mom said. "I made

tea." The double parlors in the front of the house were rarely used, even for visitors.

At the kitchen table, Wyatt's well-manicured finger traced a nick on the white enamel top that showed the rusty metal underneath. Quite different from what she must be used to in the fancy places she designed. She reached into her bag, extracting the same leather-bound journal she'd had the day before. As she turned the pages, I noticed both hand-written notes and sketches.

When my mother finally finished fussing with the tea things, she sat and I did too.

Wyatt cleared her throat. "Quentin and I had a theory even before I saw the house. You believe it was designed by Henry Gilbert but have no documentation."

"It's a family legend," Mom agreed.

"After touring the property, I concur. It will take more research, but we believe Windsholme may be Henry Gilbert's first commission. If that's true, I can't stress to you how historically significant your home is."

Mom blinked, taking in the information. "But can the house be fixed?"

Wyatt nodded. "Certainly it can and should be fixed. The question is, for what purpose? Do you plan to live in it, or is it a historic home that you offer tours through, an add-on to your clambake business? Are we renovating for modern life, or restoring it to its original condition?"

We had no answer for that. Fixing up Windsholme had never been more than a vague desire. I'd assumed that Mom would live in it, and maybe, if it could be properly divided, other members of the family as well. Maybe even Chris and me one day. The idea of treating it like a historical home had never come up.

"How much it will cost?" I asked it too sharply and Mom threw me a look I'd known since my child-hood—the look that meant she was annoyed.

"That depends on your answer to my question." Wyatt was unruffled. "Restoration will cost more than renovation, but there may be more help, like grants, tax breaks, and so on. As for the building, the foundation appears to be sound, but we'll need a full structural assessment before I can even begin to plan and estimate. That will give us time to have conver-sations about your hopes and dreams for the house— and for us all to get to know one another."

We fell silent, each of us lost in our own thoughts. I hoped Mom was beginning to understand the complexity of the task.

Wyatt gave Mom her big smile. "Jacqueline, I would so like to move forward with this work. But it will take time to do the research, do the inspec-tions, and continue these conversations so we can draw up plans and complete estimates." She took a booklet out of her portfolio. It was printed in sepia tones on heavy vellum. Wyatt opened it to a page in the middle and passed it across to my mother. "This describes my firm's services. I think what you need is a preliminary study. I'll leave this with you to review and I'll call tomorrow." Wyatt stood and Quentin did as well. "Julia, last night was lovely," she said, reminding me immediately that I should have been the one to say so, especially since we'd been rushed off the *Garbo* with no chance to say good-bye.

"It was wonderful." I found my manners. "You and . . . well . . . you, will have to come out to Morrow Island on Thursday for Family Day, the first day of the clambake." I wasn't sure whether to include Geoffrey. Did one invite a famous recluse to go on outings? Once again my manners failed me. I walked them to the door.

Mom was still at the kitchen table when I returned. Wordlessly, she handed me the booklet that described Wyatt's proposed study. Twenty thousand dollars, and before we even started.

"Isn't it great?" Mom asked, smiling. "Windsholme is potentially an architectural masterpiece. Of course, I always knew it was. You can tell by looking at it."

"*Potentially*," I emphasized. "And she wants twenty thousand dollars to figure it out." Three months earlier, before the auction of the Black Widow, a valuable necklace Mom inherited, twenty thousand dollars would have been an unthinkable amount of money.

As I'd hoped, saying the amount out loud threw on my thrifty Yankee mother's brakes. "What do you think we should do?" she asked, her brow creased.

"At a minimum, we need to meet with other firms before you spend this money. We can't go with Wyatt because Quentin knows her."

"I can't think of a better reason to hire someone," Mom countered. "Besides, you know her too."

"I knew her a little bit a long time ago."

Mom's eyes flashed. "Why do you dislike Wyatt?" When I didn't respond, she continued. "Whatever it is, it's getting in the way of you being objective."

"You're the one who's not being objective."

We weren't yelling. Only imminent mortal danger could cause my mother to yell. But we were certainly disagreeing. Vehemently.

"Okay," Mom said. "Family meeting tonight. You, me, Livvie, Sonny, Chris. Dinner."

"I hoped to stay on the island. It's only six days until we open. And Chris plans to work on the *Dark Lady*."

"Go out to the island. Get some work done, but be back for dinner."

Chapter 8

I said good-bye to Mom and went out to the front porch to enjoy the sea breeze and wait for Sonny. Across the street, a nondescript silver sedan pulled into the parking space in front of the Snuggles Inn. Maine State Police Sergeant Tom Flynn got out, walked around to the other side, and opened the passenger door for Genevieve. They both went to the trunk and pulled out two carry-on–sized rolling bags. Genevieve spotted me and waved. I waved back vigorously. She tapped Flynn on the shoulder and pointed at me. He shrugged, gave a quick smile, and turned his back.

"Come over later!" Genevieve called.

They made a striking couple. She was willowy, with glossy, short, black hair and pale, pale skin. He was good-looking enough, with military-short hair and erect posture, and a body that showed off hours spent in the gym.

Flynn turned toward the gingerbread-covered front porch of the Snuggles, put his arm around

Genevieve's shoulders, and steered her gently away from me and up the front walk. I couldn't blame him. He was desperately in love with Genevieve and he hadn't seen her in the months she'd been on the *Garbo*.

Sonny pulled into the driveway in his giant pickup. "You ready, your highness?"

"Coming."

Mom charged out the front door and straight down the steps. She stuck her face in the driver's side window, not an easy task because the truck was big and she was small. "Sonny, I'm glad to catch you. Come to dinner tonight."

Sonny drew back. "I don't know. Livvie and I were out at the concert last night."

"Come anyway. Family meeting. I want to talk this Windsholme plan through."

My mother was rarely abrupt, never rude. As a rule, she didn't order people around, and never Sonny. His face shifted and he leaned toward her. "Okay. I'll call Livvie."

"See you at six. Julia, call Chris."

I nodded my agreement and climbed up into the truck. Strictly speaking, Chris wasn't a member of the family, despite spending Thanksgiving, Christmas, and Easter with us, at my invitation. He never talked about his own family. He'd bought his cabin from his parents when they'd moved to Florida. He had an older sister in San Diego. That's all I knew. No one came to visit him and he never visited them, even when he'd gone to the Keys in February to help a buddy move a boat. Pressed, all he would say was, "There's a reason we live as far apart as we can."

I worried, early on, that my messy family life would repel him. We all worked together and were in and out of each other's homes, lives, and finances in ways it might be hard for other people to understand. Instead, my family seemed to be part of what attracted Chris to me, like he missed family life, just not his family. In any case, I knew why Mom wanted him at the meeting tonight. He'd been an early and consistent proponent of fixing up Windsholme. He was on her side.

Sonny drove the short distance to the town pier, carefully wending his way through streets crowded with more seasonal residents and tourists every day. On the pier, we each took time to make the promised phone calls about the dinner before we left the harbor and cell range. Then Sonny climbed out of his seat and went to the back of the pickup. "You ready?"

I looked into the bed and sighed. It was filled with boxes of liquor to stock the bar at the clambake. Lots of heavy lifting ahead.

Sonny and I moved the boxes to our Boston Whaler and then I waited while he drove the truck to Mom's driveway and walked back. Parking on the pier was for loading and unloading only. We were silent on the trip out to the island. Once we passed the mouth of the harbor, we wordlessly shrugged into windbreakers. Despite the bright sun, the wind coming across the Gulf of Maine was biting.

Sonny steered the boat into the dock on Morrow

Island and I tied it up. I pointed to our cargo. "Let's put the booze in the little house and lock it."

"Is that really necessary?"

I hesitated. Locking the alcohol in the house by the dock overnight would add many extra steps of fetching and hauling. My brother-in-law had been out late at a concert, then had gotten up at 4:00 AM to work on his dad's lobster boat. If I'd been able to stay on the island for the night, I wouldn't have thought twice. But the clambake bar, housed in the sprawling building that included the main dining pavilion, gift shop, and kitchen, was hard to secure. Busman's Harbor High's forty-nine seniors had already graduated, and the rest of the school would be out in a few days. It was careless to leave a mountain of alcohol unattended. "I think it is necessary. I'll get the wheelbarrow."

When we were done, Sonny took the Whaler to retrieve the first load of hardwood he'd use to fuel the clambake fire, another backbreaking job. I offered to go along, but he waved me off.

I cleared branches and debris from the walking paths, the leavings of the island's lonely winter. When we were up and running, guests arrived forty-five minutes before the clambake meal was served and were encouraged to enjoy Morrow Island. They spread out, many playing volleyball or boccie on the courts we'd laid out on Windsholme's former great lawn. Others gathered around the roaring clambake fire. There was always a good crowd watching Sonny and his crew cook the meal. Some people climbed the steep stairs to look over the ugly orange hazard fence at Windsholme and then walked through the woods to the two-room playhouse that was a replica of the mansion. The hardiest guests hiked up over the hill all the way to the little beach on the other side of the island.

I walked with a rake in one hand and a broom in the other. When I reached the beach, I stood still for a moment and stared at Quentin's black marble and glass house rising out of the rocks on the other side of the channel. His sleek, carbon-fiber sailboat, the *Flittermouse*, bobbed at its dock, but his antique woody wasn't in the driveway. Where was he? What was his relationship to Wyatt? I had no doubt they were acquaintances, but I'd never known Quentin to have friends, at least not in the classic sense. The challenge of getting to know him had been frustrating. I wanted to be his friend.

I went back up the hill and stood, staring at the ugly hazard fence and Windsholme's boarded-up facade behind it. The silhouette of the mansion was one of the enduring images of my life. I tried to imagine the space empty, the view from where I stood over the cliffs to the sea. Once Windsholme was gone, would we forget it quickly, as if it had never been? Or would it always be with us, a ghostly outline never coming into focus?

Mom was taken with Wyatt. My mother was shy and New England–reserved. She didn't usually make judgments about people so quickly. Was it something about Wyatt, or was it simply her potential to give my mother what she wanted, a giant piece of her childhood preserved? Rebuilding Windsholme would have to take place in good weather. It would be disruptive to the clambake business, so I'd have to work closely with whoever was in charge. Could I stomach months, maybe years, of Wyatt Jayne?

The years fell away and I was my teenage self, shy and uncertain again. Wyatt and her friends were hanging out in our dorm room, something they did nearly every evening before dinner. They ignored me and I tried my best to ignore them, bending over my homework at my narrow desk.

"Ms. Davis is the best," Melissa cooed. "I went to her for help with my essay and she couldn't have been nicer."

Most often, they complained about our teachers, who were, according to Wyatt and her friends, irritating, vague, and boring. They had bad breath, bad hair, and bad posture. But they all loved our English teacher, Ms. Davis. I loved her too.

"We should do something for her," Wyatt said.

"We could give her candy," Lainey suggested.

"Too fattening." Wyatt had a point. Ms. Davis was young and slender. She, her husband, and their toddler daughter lived in an apartment in one of the boys' dorms.

"Apples?" Lainey tried again. "We could pick them at the orchard down the road."

Wyatt shot that down too. "She gets all her meals in the dining hall."

"Offer to babysit for her kid so she and her husband could have a date night," I suggested.

Wyatt looked at me with interest. "More like that. But I want to spend time with Ms. Davis."

"Invite her to a nice lunch at the inn," I said. "That way, she gets a break and there's plenty of time for conversation."

"That's it!" Wyatt cried, looking at me with new, much more impressed eyes. "What a good idea. We'll *all* take her to lunch."

Sonny lumbered up beside me, causing me to jump as my mind jerked back to the present. "Sorry," he said. "Didn't mean to scare you. I'm back."

"So I see." Sonny stared at the boarded-up facade of Windsholme. "What do you think we should do about it?" I asked him.

He used a freckled forearm to wipe his freckled brow. "I wasn't aware there was a 'we' involved. Your mother's house, your mother's money, right?"

"She's called a family meeting. She must want our opinions." I told him what Wyatt had said that morning. He whistled when I mentioned the amount for the study.

He shifted onto his back foot, his big barrel chest a wall beside me. "Can you really imagine people coming to the island to tour the house?"

I hesitated. "I can, I guess. We'd have to furnish it appropriately. Maybe we could all wear costumes and pretend we were living in 1892."

"I'd rather be shot."

I laughed. I didn't doubt it. "I know. I'm teasing. Let's not do that. What do you really think?"

"To the extent it's my business, I'd much rather pay off what we owe Quentin, invest in the clambake, and put the rest away for a rainy day."

"And Windsholme?"

"Tear it down."

"I agree." That's what I wanted too, though I thought of it always as "not rebuilding." The phrase "tear it down" had such bald brutality and finality, it stabbed me in the heart. I took a deep breath, pushing the pain away. I had to be practical because Mom wouldn't be. "Let's get going. We have Family Day coming up fast."

Sonny grunted. "At least we aren't starting the season with an effing wedding for your friends this year."

I looked at my bear of a brother-in-law. He and I had fought all through the previous clambake season, starting with my idea to hold more private events, including a wedding for a New York City acquaintance. That's when I'd first invested in Windsholme, decorating and rewiring two rooms to serve as a staging area and dressing room for the bridal party. That small decision had led inexorably to the fire that had damaged the mansion to the point where we were considering tearing it down.

Sonny had viewed me coming home to run the clambake business as a slap in his face, a statement about his failure. To some extent it had been, though the banking crisis, recession, and seasons of lousy weather hadn't helped. As I tried to rescue the business he'd taken every change I made as a personal affront.

But about the future of Windsholme—we were on the same side. What would that be like?

Chapter 9

Eight of us sat around the formal dining room table—Mom at the head; Chris, me, and Livvie on one side; Sonny, Page, and Vanessa on the other. Baby Jack dozed peacefully in his car seat at the far end of the table, occasionally rubbing his tiny nose. The rest of us still avoided my dad's seat when there was room elsewhere.

Sonny and I had stayed on Morrow as long as we could, cutting it close. When we'd entered Mom's house I'd inhaled deeply. The smell of Livvie's go-to, hurry-up meal, Beer-Can Chicken, filled the room. Livvie and Chris were bent over the stove, conferring about the potatoes.

Chris and I didn't have time to strategize. He'd given me a quick peck on the cheek as I'd dashed for a shower. I assumed we'd come out on different sides when my mother started the discussion about what to do with Windsholme, and the chips would fall where they might.

The children's presence at the table guaranteed the

conversation wouldn't take place during dinner, so we were free to enjoy the meal. My mother was a terrible cook. I was the only person I knew who never pined for her mother's cooking. Livvie, on the other hand, was wonderful. Her Beer-Can Chicken was full of flavor and fell off the bone. And the roasted potatoes . . . I closed my eyes, shutting down my other senses so I could fully appreciate their taste and perfect texture. I was glad the Windsholme discussion had to wait. I didn't want it to interfere with our enjoyment of the meal.

I'd raised an eyebrow at Livvie after I'd come through the back door and spotted Vanessa helping Page set the table. "Her mother took a double at Crowley's again today," Livvie explained. "Mom's helping out, having the girls sleep over again tonight."

It didn't surprise me that Vanessa's mother had grabbed another shift. Most people in Busman's Harbor crammed as much income as they could into the short months of the season. Crowley's was Busman's Harbor's busiest, most touristy bar. On a Friday in June, working two shifts would be exhausting. It also didn't surprise me that my quiet, formal, yet big-hearted mother was pitching in to support a relative stranger.

At the table, we chatted about our days. It was an easy conversation filled with tasks accomplished and plans for the summer. Once the clambake opened, we wouldn't have dinner at this table for the rest of the season. The meal we served on Morrow Island, in the lull after the lunch guests left and before the dinner guests arrived, was called the family meal, but it included all our employees, our extended summer family. It was one of my favorite times of the day, but it wasn't this.

Several times during the meal, I caught Chris staring at Vanessa, his green eyes seeking hers, like animals that recognize a fellow member of their species. It wasn't the time or the place to ask him about it.

After dinner, the girls excused themselves to play on the front porch. "Strawberry shortcake in a little while," Livvie told them. "I'll call you." The grown-ups stayed at the dining room table, lingering over coffee.

"As you all know, I'm facing a decision about what to do with Windsholme," my mother began after we'd settled. She told the others pretty accurately what Wyatt had said—I had to admit, not tilting it one way or the other. "As I see it, my options are to restore it as a historical site, renovate it so some or all of us can live in it during the summer, or tear it down. I don't think there's an option to leave it as is. It's an eyesore and will become increasingly dangerous. It's my decision, but I want your thoughts. I can't promise to go along with whatever you suggest, but I do promise to listen."

She looked across the table at Sonny. He knew what my mother wanted, but he'd been a member of the family since he and Livvie had fallen in love in high school, working, laughing, and grieving with us, so he spoke his mind. "It's no secret. I think Windsholme should be torn down. It'll be expensive to get the equipment out to the island and haul the trash off, but not as expensive as either of the other options. People come to the island for the clambake. We've never used the house as a part of the operation. We don't need another attraction." At this last he pulled his head up, looking at my mother straight on.

She nodded to show she had heard. "Livvie."

Like her husband, Livvie spoke in a low, even voice. "I think Windsholme should be restored. Wyatt says it's a historic building. And we're lucky enough to have a living member of the family who was there in the old days and who can help guide the restoration. We can't count on that much longer." She meant my mother's cousin Marguerite, who was in her midnineties. My mother hadn't known of her existence until the previous winter, and Marguerite hadn't seen Windsholme in more than eighty years. She'd promised to visit Morrow Island this summer, but no one knew if she'd be up to the trip.

"Restoring is the most expensive route of all. And, it would have to be furnished in period pieces, another expense," I said.

"You'll get your turn," my mother cautioned.

"We have something special. Special to our town, to American architecture, and to our family," Livvie concluded. "If we lose it, it's gone forever."

My mother moved on. "Chris."

"I'm not a member of the family," Chris said. "But if you want my opinion, it's still what it was before Wyatt arrived. Windsholme should be updated so some or all of you can live there comfortably in the summer. Livvie and Sonny's family fills the little house by the dock. There's no practical way anyone else can stay overnight." He looked at me, instead of my mother. "You love Morrow Island, and you'll want to stay there someday with your own family. You've all been given a chance, a one in a million shot, to reclaim this house. Don't turn it into a dusty museum. Enjoy it as a family. That's why your ancestors built it."

My mother allowed a hint of a smile, then wiped it away. She wasn't fooling anyone. Chris's opinion most closely matched her own. "Julia."

I was next to her at the table. She had to angle herself to look at me. The sun had set while we talked, leaving a violet sky visible through the diamond-shaped panes in the high dining room windows. We hadn't turned on the chandelier and I was grateful for the shadows.

"It's a hard decision," I acknowledged. "And I think it's too early to make it. We don't have costs yet for any of the three options. When we get them, one or more may turn out to be impossible."

"We'll have to pay Wyatt for the study to find out. Twenty thousand dollars," Mom reminded.

"Wyatt's or some other firm," I responded. "I'm not convinced she's the one. It would be smart to interview more people. But yes, I do think the prudent thing is to go to the next stage, find out what each of the options involves."

Sonny glared at me. I was supposed to be on his side and was taking the coward's way out. "If you had to decide today, what would you do?" he demanded. "Put a stake in the ground like the rest of us."

"If I had to decide today . . ." I hesitated. And then I was saved by the chirping of my cell phone, which I'd left recharging on the buffet. I got up to take a look at the screen. My mother glowered. I wouldn't normally have answered, but it was Wyatt. She might have something relevant to say about the current discussion. "Excuse me." I went through the swinging doorway into the kitchen, phone clutched to my ear.

"Julia—" Her voice was shaky and loud.

"Wyatt? Are you all right?"

"No. Please come to the *Garbo*. Now. Something terrible has happened."

"Have you called nine-one-one?"

"Not yet. I'm too scared. I called Quentin, but he lives so far away. I need someone quickly." She was crying, great stuttering gasps. I could barely understand her.

"Wyatt? What's going on? Talk to me."

No answer.

"Wyatt, I'm on my way. I'm bringing Chris. Do you want me to call nine-one-one and tell them you're in trouble?"

"No! No! Just come. As fast as you can. Please."

It would take about the same amount of time to drive around the harbor to the other side as it would to run across the footbridge, but after a hurried consult with Chris, we grabbed his pickup. Wyatt might need a ride to the hospital. Chris's legendary lead foot left tourists scattering as we sped across town.

We ran through Blount's, down the wooden stairs to the floating dock, and up the *Garbo*'s gangway.

"Wyatt! Wyatt! Where are you?"

A strangled sound echoed from a deck somewhere above. I spotted her outside the dining salon. We raced to her. She was a wreck. Pale, shaking, crying, clutching her stomach.

"What is it, Wyatt? What's wrong?"

She straightened up and, silently, still shaking, led us into the dining room. At the head of the table, Geoffrey Bower sat motionless, wearing the same yachtsman's cap and blue blazer as the day before, his face contorted in a horrible grimace.

Chris ran toward Bower. Wyatt doubled over, hysterical. I took her in my arms. "What's happened? Tell me." I looked over her toward Chris, who silently shook his head. I crouched down to meet her eyes. "Wyatt, honey, we need to call nine-one-one. Chris will do it while I stay with you."

"Geoffrey will hate that," she whispered. "Hate having all those strangers on board." She couldn't go on.

"We have to," I said firmly. "Let's go."

The sooner we got away from that horrible sight, the better. Before we left, I scanned the room, trying to commit everything to memory. There would be lots of questions later. Looking away from Geoffrey and his contorted, jack-o'-lantern grin, I saw the table was laid for a sumptuous cold supper, just as Genevieve had described the night before. The centerpiece was a red lobster body, holding out his claw. Clutched in it was something so surprising, I took a second look to be sure of what I'd seen—a ring with a large, sparkling diamond.

Chapter 10

I hustled Wyatt to the deck as she gulped for air. Behind us, Chris closed the double doors to the dining salon and stood in front of them, arms crossed. I kept moving with Wyatt, down toward the dock. We reached the top of the gangway just as Quentin ran up it. He stared at the bent over, distraught figure of Wyatt. "What's going on?"

I shook my head, not wanting to describe the gruesome scene in Wyatt's presence. "Chris is above. He'll fill you in." Quentin ran on.

I wasn't sure what to do. I didn't want to leave Wyatt under the dock lights where anyone could see her, but we had to stay nearby. We started up the steps toward Blount's.

Jamie and Officer Howland were the first to arrive. "Where?" Jamie demanded as they passed us on the patio. I pointed to the yacht. "Chris and Quentin are there, outside the dining room, third level."

"Wait inside," Jamie commanded.

The manager of Blount's had come out, drawn by the cops running through his lobby for the second day in a row.

"Is there a conference room where we can wait?" I asked him.

He appeared at first not to understand the question, but then he looked at Wyatt and comprehension dawned. "Of course." He barked for a bellhop to show us the way. Before we followed him down the hallway, two EMTs ran through the lobby with a stretcher. I could have told them it was pointless, but I kept silent.

The handsome protester ran into the lobby. He grabbed my arm as we passed. "What's happening?" he demanded. The color drained from his face as he watched the EMTs board the *Garbo*.

I shook my head, not prepared to answer, and moved past him. The bellhop led the way to a ground-floor conference room; I followed with my arm around Wyatt. The windows were high on the walls. I was grateful Wyatt couldn't see what was going on outside. The bellhop bustled around, turning on the lights and fetching a pitcher of ice water from behind the bar. Then he left us alone. I steered Wyatt to one of the comfortable chairs surrounding the conference table. I poured her a glass of water, retrieved a box of tissues from the adjacent powder room, and sat down.

Chris and Quentin arrived within minutes. When he opened the door to let them in to the conference room, Officer Howland barked, "No comparing notes about what you saw or heard!" He needn't have worried. None of us were inclined to discuss any of it in front of Wyatt in her current state.

And then we waited. Chris and Quentin took turns walking out to the lobby, returning with reports about the activity. "EMTs are gone." "State police car is here." The next people to arrive were Sergeant Flynn and Genevieve. He was dressed in a crisply ironed, short-sleeved shirt and dress pants, obviously off duty. Genevieve was in a cute summer dress and a little cardigan. They must have been at dinner. Flynn made sure Genevieve was settled and then walked out, no doubt eager to find out what was happening.

He returned and sat next to Genevieve. "They're here," he said.

Wyatt looked up at him. "Who?"

"State police detectives, including my partner, Lieutenant Binder, and"—he hesitated, but went on—"technicians from the state medical examiner's office."

That was too much information for Wyatt, who broke down again. I handed her tissues and she fought for control.

Finally, the door opened, and Lieutenant Jerry Binder walked in. He greeted those whom he knew, which was everyone except Wyatt. To her he said, "Ms. Jayne, I presume?" He stood at the front of the room and spoke. He wasn't a big man, or a particularly handsome one, with his ski-slope nose and the fringe of light brown hair around his bald head. But when he spoke, it was with an authority that demanded you listen. "Either I, or one of my colleagues from the state police Major Crimes Unit will interview each of you shortly. With Ms. Pelletier's help, we've made contact with all but one of the *Garbo*'s crew members. They should be arriving as they can. We've made arrangements for the crew to stay here at Blount's, except for Genevieve, who has accommodations elsewhere." I noticed he used her given name that time. She was his partner's girlfriend, after all. Binder turned toward Wyatt. "Ms. Jayne, I understand you found Mr. Bower. We'll see you first." His tone was gentle, even kind.

Wyatt nodded miserably and made her way slowly toward Binder, who showed her out. Sergeant Flynn didn't move from his seat. "You're not on the case?" I asked.

He shook his head. "Genevieve's a crew member. I picked her up from the *Garbo* this morning."

"Do they have a particular interest in the crew?"

"Julia—" His voice held a warning, but then he relaxed. "I doubt it. At this point, it's standard procedure."

While Binder interviewed Wyatt, members of the crew filtered into Blount's conference room. First came Ian, the Australian deckhand; Doug, the pale engineer; and Rick, the French head steward. They told us they'd been at Crowley's, and from the smell of them, they certainly had been drinking. Emil, the bodyguard, and Marius, the captain, arrived about an hour later. They said they'd been in Portland, enjoying a nice meal in a restaurant when they got the call. They had hotel rooms in the city's Old Port district and had planned to stay overnight. Only Maria Consuelo, the young stewardess, wasn't there. Genevieve had explained to the police that Maria Consuelo didn't have a cell phone, and since she apparently wasn't with any other member of the crew, she was unreachable. The police would have to wait for her to turn up.

Chris and I were interviewed after Wyatt, which made sense since we'd been the second ones to arrive at the crime scene. Jamie came to get us, taking us behind the front desk to a suite of hotel offices. He deposited Chris in the first room and walked me to the next one. Lieutenant Binder and the second detective, whoever he was, must have interviewed Wyatt together. Now they were splitting up to talk to Chris and me. Binder answered Jamie's soft rap on the door. "Come in."

The office was larger than I'd expected. It must have been the manager's. Binder rose from behind the desk and motioned me to a seat opposite. "Julia. We meet in unpleasant circumstances, once again."

"We do." There was no point in denying it.

"Why don't you walk me through the events of the evening."

I told him about Wyatt's call.

"And your relationship to Ms. Jayne is . . . ?"

"We went to prep school together. Many years ago. I hadn't seen her again until yesterday. Quentin recommended her to my mother as an architect for a project we're considering on Morrow Island."

"Why did she call you when she discovered Mr. Bower?"

"She called Quentin Tupper first. They *are* friends, apparently. But then she realized how long it would take him to drive over from Westclaw Point, and she panicked. I guess I'm the only other person she knows in town."

I told him about how Chris and I had rushed over to the *Garbo*. In a series of questions, he took me through what I'd seen, what I'd touched. What Wyatt had said. What Chris had said. He put on a pair of reading glasses I'd never seen him wear before and typed into his laptop as I spoke.

"There was a meal laid out on the table. Bower was behind it with that hideous smile." I closed my eyes, trying to blot it out, but that just made the image stronger. I shook my head and opened them again.

"How did you know it was Bower?"

"We had dinner with him on the yacht last night."

He made a note on the laptop. I assumed Wyatt would have already told him about the dinner. He led me through the night before, probing for details, occasionally nodding, still taking notes. Then he sat back in his chair and took off the glasses. "Why didn't Ms. Jayne call nine-one-one right away? Why call Tupper and you?"

"I'd be speculating if I answered."

"I'm asking you to speculate."

"Geoffrey Bower was a recluse. He never left the ship. I think, in her panic, Wyatt wanted to shield him. Of course, she couldn't. As soon as we saw . . . what we saw, Chris made the call."

"Did you meet the crew last night when you were aboard?"

"Yes. I hadn't realized Genevieve Pelletier worked for Bower, but once we found out, she invited us down to the crew quarters. Chris and Quentin had a tour of the mechanicals with Doug, the engineer, and Genevieve showed me the galley."

"Tell me about Wyatt Jayne's relationship with the victim," Binder said.

"I'm not sure what I can tell you. Until yesterday, I hadn't seen Wyatt since high school."

"How did they act toward one another?"

My sense had been that Wyatt cared more about winning, or keeping, Geoffrey's affection than he cared about winning hers, yet Geoffrey was the one who'd asked the crew to shove off for the night. "All I know is, Wyatt referred to Geoffrey as her boyfriend," I answered. "And there was the diamond ring."

"The what?" Binder said it casually, not looking up from the laptop where he was typing.

"The ring with the big diamond that was clutched in the lobster's claw, on the dining table in front of Geoffrey Bower's corpse."

I had his attention. "There was no diamond ring on the table, in a lobster's claw or any other place."

Now he had mine. "I'm positive there was."

Binder didn't speak for several seconds. "After you left the dining salon with Ms. Jayne"—he scrolled back through his notes—"Mr. Durand stayed to guard the crime scene while you took her down to the main deck and ultimately off the ship."

"Yes," I confirmed.

"How long was Mr. Durand alone above decks?"

"I don't know. Maybe five minutes. Quentin Tupper showed up as Wyatt and I were leaving the *Garbo* and I sent him up to wait with Chris." I held up my hand, palm out. "Don't even consider Chris might have taken it," I told him. Binder and Chris had had problems in the past.

"That isn't my assumption. Excuse me." Binder left the room, no doubt to pass the information about the diamond to the detective who was interviewing Chris.

When he returned, I described the ring and its setting, in detail and without hesitation.

"You remember it clearly for something you saw for a few moments, tops."

I hesitated. "Yes." I didn't tell Lieutenant Binder I thought I'd seen the diamond before. It sounded too nuts. I remembered it because I'd recognized it. Or at least, I thought I did.

Chris and I drove back to our apartment over the quiet streets of Busman's Harbor. The bars were closed.

Everyone seemed to have returned to their hotel rooms and to bed.

"How'd it go?"

"Fine," I said.

"They asked a lot of questions about Wyatt," he noted.

"Isn't that always the way? They look at the significant other."

"I couldn't tell them much. I met her yesterday."

"Me either. I hadn't seen her since high school graduation. Until yesterday."

We rode in silence for a minute. The streetlights of Main Street slid by.

"You don't like her," Chris said.

"I like her fine."

"Julia . . ." He wasn't buying it.

"All right. I didn't like her in high school and I haven't made up my mind whether I like her now. Can we drop it?"

"Consider it dropped."

When we passed Mom's house, the lights were off, the windows silent pools of black. The girls must have gone to bed willingly.

"Did you see a diamond ring on the table in the dining room?" I tried to keep my voice light, an offhand inquiry about a detail.

He pulled the truck into the parking lot at Gus's. The windows to our apartment upstairs were as dark as the others in town. "Nope. The detective asked me about a ring too. I told him the same thing. Didn't see it. Honestly, Julia, I couldn't notice much beyond that awful smile of Geoffrey's." He opened the door to the truck, but didn't get out. In the dome light, I could see his rugged profile, his broad shoulders. I fell against his chest and he wrapped his strong arms around me.

"It's going to be okay," was all he said.

Chapter 11

In the morning I woke up to the chirp of my cell phone. I glanced at the screen. Mom. It was after nine o'clock. I'd slept in without intending to. The other side of the bed was empty. Chris had a lot to do before his landscaping clients arrived in town, and after that he was working a Saturday night shift at Crowley's. Even the late night, crazy events at Blount's hadn't kept him in bed.

I answered the phone.

"Oh, good. I need a favor." Mom started without even a hello. "Can you run Vanessa home? I don't want to be late for work since it's my last day for the summer."

I had over an hour before I was supposed to meet Livvie and her family to go out to Morrow Island. "Sure. Where does she live?"

"On Thistle Island. I'm sorry. I know you're busy."

Thistle Island was not an island like Morrow. It was connected to Busman's Harbor by a swing bridge, a bridge that opened, turning on a central pivot, to allow boat traffic to pass through. Thistle was in the opposite direction from Mom's job at Linens and Pantries in Topsham. It was the first job Mom had held outside the Snowden family business since before I was born. She'd gotten off to a rough start, baffled by the technology and the sheer size of the place, but she'd found her feet and been promoted to assistant manager in the spring. She hoped to return after the clambake closed in the fall, and she wouldn't want to leave on a low note.

"What's happening with Page?" I asked.

"She has her swim team picnic today. It's on my way."

"Give me ten minutes."

Mom met me on the front porch, car keys in her hand. "What happened with Wyatt last night after you and Chris ran out of here? Why didn't you *call*?"

"Sorry. It got late." I took her hand. "Mom, Geoffrey Bower died last night. Wyatt discovered his body."

My mother's mouth fell open, followed by a sharp intake of breath. "That poor girl. Was it a heart attack? A stroke?"

The awful rictus grin on Geoffrey's corpse rose out of my memory, unbidden. "Lieutenant Binder's in town along with a team from the Major Crimes Unit."

That stopped Mom short. "They think it was murder? That poor, poor girl." Mom took her hand from mine, glancing at the delicate watch on her wrist as she did. "I have to go. Girls!"

Page and Vanessa hustled out the door. Vanessa was in the same shorts and T-shirt she'd worn the evening before. She'd made a partially successful attempt to detangle her long brown hair. The rest of her tiny features made the big, deep-set green eyes seem bigger and more haunting.

We had a brief tussle when she tried to climb into the front seat of the ancient Chevy Caprice I kept stored in Mom's garage.

"My mom lets me," she protested when I shooed her to the backseat.

"I don't care what your mom does. In my car, you ride in the back." Sometimes even when you don't have kids, you turn into your own mother.

Vanessa was quiet on the ride until we got to the swing bridge, where I asked her whether to go right or left on the road that ringed Thistle Island.

"Left." Her voice was so soft, I had to strain to hear, but the single word loosened her tongue. "If you tear down Windsholme, where will the ghost live?"

Evidently the girls had overheard more of the previous night's discussion than the adults intended. I had to think for a moment about that one. "I don't think ghosts need houses exactly."

"But you said she's waiting for her lover." She pronounced the word "lover" without irony, but even that sounded strange coming from a child. "If the house is gone, he won't know where to go. How will they find each other?"

I had no answer for that, so we rode in silence for a moment.

"Why didn't she have her own house?" Vanessa asked.

"Who?"

"Lenora Bailey. Why did she live with your family?"

I didn't know beyond the basics. In 1892 domestic help lived in, or at least they did if you were a rich family who lived on an island. But what had Lenora's circumstances been? Was she a local girl, or maybe a recent immigrant? Did she travel with my family from their home in Boston, or only work for them during the summer?

"Turn here."

"What?"

"Turn right here. That's our driveway."

The Caprice struggled up a steep, dirt drive to a flat spot where an old trailer stood next to a ramshackle cottage. In the rearview mirror, across the ring road, I could see a dense wood with a gate at the start of a well-kept gravel driveway. Through those woods, there would be a big house with magnificent views of Townsend Bay and a deep-water dock for a large motorboat or sailboat. Maybe both.

I'd sailed those waters all my life, and I didn't have to see the house to know it was there. Over the past two generations almost all the waterfront in the county had been bought by affluent summer people and rich retirees who had built or renovated beautiful homes, sited to capture the views. But less than a quarter mile away from some of those homes, on lots without views, stood places like this trailer,

sheltering lives of constant struggle. Thistle Island
was like a juicy peach, beautiful and inviting on the
outside, with a hard pit at the center.

I heard Vanessa's seat belt click open as I turned
off the Caprice's engine. "Which one is yours?" I
asked, indicating the trailer and the cottage. "I want
to make sure your mom knows you're here."

"That one." Vanessa pointed to the trailer. "The
house is my mom's grandma's. We used to have a
house of our own, but we had to move."

A woman with a cute, round face and curly blond
hair appeared in the trailer's doorway. She wore a
short robe and held a chubby baby in her arms. She
was small like Vanessa and maybe my age.

"Mom!" Vanessa bolted, running toward her
mother.

"Whoa." She smiled at her daughter, putting out
her other hand to stop a collision. "Thank you for
bringing her," she called to me. "And thank your mom
and sister."

I left the car door open and walked toward her.
"You're welcome. I'm Julia, by the way."

"Emmy Bailey. Pleased to meet you."

"Same here."

She nodded with her chin toward the baby, who
blew a bubble. "My grandma can handle him, but
not both of them. Besides, Vanessa loves Page so
much." The baby's eyes were blue, not green.

"I'm sure my mom was happy to do it." Even as I
said it, I wondered what this woman's plans were for
the rest of the season. Mom wouldn't be able to help
with child care once she was back at the shop on

Morrow Island. Our tour boat didn't return to town until ten o'clock, after the second seating finished dinner. "I think you might know my boyfriend. He works at Crowley's too. Chris Durand."

Emmy blinked. "Is that his last name? We've only worked the same shift once or twice. I guess I'll see more of him once the season gets going."

I said my good-byes and turned back toward my car, waving at Vanessa, who was hanging on a rusty swing set. Back in the Caprice, I laughed at myself for my stupid suspicions. Emmy hadn't even known Chris's name. I drove carefully down the steep drive and back to Busman's Harbor.

On the way home, the swing bridge was open. I was the fifth car in line as we waited for a majestic sailboat to glide through, leaving the salt water of the back harbor for the brackish and ultimately fresh water of Townsend Bay. My phone pinged with a text. Livvie. **RUNNING LATE WILL MEET U NOON.** *Great.* But with a baby, Livvie wasn't the master of her time.

Quentin sat on my mother's porch as I pulled in her driveway. I put the Caprice in its usual spot in Mom's sagging and too short garage, and walked around to the front of the house to greet him.

"Quentin."

He started and looked toward me. His mind must have been somewhere else. "May I have a word?" he asked.

"Of course." I stepped inside the porch, closing

the screen door behind us. I gestured toward the sturdy rattan furniture with its old, flowered cushions.

Quentin took a seat on the sofa and I sat across from him on one of the generously proportioned chairs. He put his elbows on his knees and looked at me, his blue eyes made brighter by his rich-man's tan. He had the coloring of someone who could afford to chase summer across the globe. But there was no mistaking the worry in his eyes. "Will you help her?" he asked.

He meant Wyatt. "What makes you think she needs help?"

He exhaled heavily, his shoulders rising and falling. "C'mon, Julia. Lieutenant Binder asked me more questions about Wyatt last night than he did about Bower."

"You know Wyatt better than Bower. Better than anyone else in town does." I put my hand on his forearm. His skin was warm. "They always focus on the significant other first. Once they're satisfied Wyatt had no reason to kill Geoffrey, they'll move on."

"Maybe, maybe not. From what she told me, Binder put her through the wringer last night. She's sure they suspect her."

I removed my hand. "But you don't."

He grimaced in exasperation. "C'mon, Julia. I know you and Wyatt have this *thing*, but you don't think she could kill anyone, do you?"

"We don't have a *thing*," I protested. "I haven't seen her in thirteen years. How would I know what she is and isn't capable of?"

"You do have a thing. A high school thing. When

she's around, you're tight as a guitar string ready to snap. Do you seriously think because she beat you out for captain of the debate team, or whatever, Wyatt is capable of murder?"

"Of course not."

"Then help her."

Across the street at the Snuggles Inn, the heavy mahogany front door opened and Sergeant Tom Flynn appeared on the porch. He was dressed in jeans and a maroon T-shirt, which meant he was still off the case. He strode off toward the old stable behind the inn that served as the Snuggles storage facility and garage.

Quentin watched me watching Flynn. "Even if I wanted to, what makes you think I can help her?" I asked him.

"You've assisted both Binder and Flynn in the past. They know you. They trust you. Or, at least, Binder does. You can find out what they're thinking. And you can help prove Wyatt is innocent. Steer them in another direction."

"Why? Why do you want me to help her? What's the story with you two?"

"Wyatt's been a friend for a long time. A good friend." His eyes sought mine and held them, looking for comprehension. "Please."

Quentin was my friend too, and part owner of my business. Though he could buy and sell me a hundred times over, he'd always treated me as an equal. It was impossible to say no, so I attempted to set some ground rules. "Okay, but Wyatt's got to meet with me and tell me everything she knows."

He nodded. "Agreed. Though I didn't tell her I was going to ask you, so let me talk to her first."

I grunted. Maybe this whole request would come to nothing. Across the street, Flynn reappeared lugging something heavy and awkward. A swing. He set it down on the porch.

I turned back to Quentin. "And you too. You're going to have to tell me everything you know. Everything."

"I will. I promise. But right now, I've got to get to the police station. Wyatt's being questioned again and I want to be there when she gets out. We'll talk later. And thank you." He stood, then bent and gave me a peck on cheek. He went through the screen door, climbed down the front steps, and walked off without looking back.

I called after him, "Don't thank me yet."

Chapter 12

I watched Quentin go down Mom's walk, turn left, and head toward town. I wasn't sure about his plea to help Wyatt. I'd been involved in too many police investigations since I'd come back to Busman's Harbor, for one. And, until two days before, I hadn't seen Wyatt since she'd been called up to the podium a dozen times to receive awards and recognitions at our prep school graduation. I had a business to start up for the season and I didn't owe her anything.

On the other hand, it was Quentin who had asked, not Wyatt. And I had my own reason for being interested. The diamond ring. I was deeply curious about its origins, and whether it drew a line, even a convoluted one, between Geoffrey Bower and me.

Across the street, Flynn appeared around the corner from the back of the Snuggles Inn again, this time carrying a ladder. He set it up on the front porch and prepared to hang the swing.

The inn's owners, the Snugg sisters, had a way of

getting their B&B guests to do chores. That people would drive up from the city, do a bunch of annoying but necessary household tasks, and actually pay the Snuggs for the privilege had always confounded me. The sisters were charming, no doubt. And, since they were well into their seventies, some of the heavier lifting that had to be done around the inn was out of the question for them. I thought maybe they reminded their guests of some aged relative, a beloved grandmother now gone, to whom they could never say no. Whatever the reason, guests returned to the Snuggles year after year to wash the windows, scrub the beautiful oak floors, or put out the porch furniture. They just did. It was a kind of Snugg sister magic.

Flynn wasn't a regular guest, though the sisters had a soft spot for Genevieve, who had stayed with them before. They also had an admiration for Sergeant Flynn's muscles, both from an aesthetic and practical point of view, and obviously hadn't been able to resist putting him to work.

I hesitated, but not long, and then headed across the street.

"Julia." Flynn gave me a curt nod as he set up the ladder.

"Sergeant."

"I'm Tom today." Our relationship had been tense in the beginning. He'd disapproved of the way Lieutenant Binder sometimes took my advice or gave me information. But over Christmas, Flynn and I had worked on a case while the lieutenant was on vacation, and Flynn's attitude toward me had softened.

"So last night was wild," I said.

"Yup," he agreed. "Genevieve got the call about Bower when we were halfway through dinner. Not the romantic evening I'd planned." Flynn was up on the ladder. I squinted to make out his expression in the shadow of the porch ceiling. The elegant ginger-bread framing the structure scrolled behind his head, filtering the high June sun. I untangled the heavy chain and handed one end of it up to him. I lifted the swing as he attempted to get the link over the hook in the ceiling.

"You have your sources," I continued. "Have you heard anything?"

Flynn looked down at me. "I suppose there's no chance of you staying out of this." He successfully hooked the chain and came down the ladder. "No, I didn't think so. I'll tell you what I know, if it will keep you out of Lieutenant Binder's hair, but you can't tell anyone where this came from."

"Agreed."

"And one other thing. You'll tell me what you find out."

This was something new. In the past, Flynn had been uninterested in any information I had to offer. Evidently things were different when he too was on the outside.

Flynn moved the ladder under the other hook and climbed up. "At this point, they're waiting for the autopsy, but proceeding as if Bower's death is a homicide."

"I noticed, but how could they come to that conclusion so quickly?"

Flynn grunted as I lifted the swing toward him. "Definitely homicide. Something he ingested. They're still testing to find out what. According to the medical examiner, he'd been dead three, maybe four hours, when Ms. Jayne found him. Or when she said she found him."

"You think she's lying?"

He shrugged. "Anybody might be lying."

"She seemed genuinely hysterical to me."

"The key word being 'seemed.' It's way too early to speculate."

He slipped the second chain over the hook and the swing moved gently on its own. It was one of my favorite places to sit on a summer day. Not that there'd be much, or even any, sitting around once the clambake was open.

Flynn moved back down the ladder like a lithe cat. He was a fitness freak, rigid about what he ate and religious about his running and gym routines. I grinned appreciatively at the sight of his muscled torso. He noticed me noticing and I blushed.

"Who was the last person to see Bower alive?" I asked.

"I don't know. I picked Genevieve up at the *Garbo* at ten thirty yesterday morning. According to Vieve the rest of the crew were planning to leave throughout the day. Days off are rare on a yacht with a full-time owner aboard. Everyone wanted to take advantage for some R and R."

"If Genevieve left the *Garbo* more than four hours before Bower died, doesn't that put her in the clear, and you back on the case?"

"No, because Bower died from something he ingested. Genevieve left the food for both lunch yesterday and the dinner last night in the refrigerator, all laid out on platters. He could have eaten it at any time." Flynn caught my eyes and held them. I nodded. I got it. "Or, maybe that's not how it happened at all," he continued. "They're testing all the food. We don't know at this point. *I* don't know at this point. Bower has no family. His lawyer is on the way to town. I suppose the team will know more after they talk to him. And once they figure out what killed Bower."

Flynn closed the ladder. "Got to take this upstairs. There's a bulb out in the overhead light in room six. Do we have a deal? Is there anything you're not telling me?"

"Last night I saw a diamond ring on the table in front of Bower's body," I told him.

Flynn nodded. I had the sense it wasn't new information. "You told the lieutenant about it."

"Yes, but I'm not sure he believed me. Chris didn't see it and it wasn't there when Lieutenant Binder arrived. As far as I know, it's still missing."

Flynn put his arm through the ladder and hefted it onto his shoulder. "The lieutenant usually believes you." He fixed me with a penetrating stare, the kind that would have intimidated me a few short months before. "Is that it?"

"Yes." I wasn't going to tell him the other thing I knew about the diamond ring yet. Not until I was sure.

Flynn and the ladder disappeared inside. The screen door opened again and Vee Snugg stood there, elegant as always in hose and high heels, her crisply ironed cotton dress protected by an equally crisply ironed white bib apron.

"I thought I heard your voice, Julia. Wonderful timing. I've been teaching Genevieve to bake my ginger scones and they're fresh out of the oven. Let's have some tea."

I sat at the Snugg sisters' wooden kitchen table with its familiar nicks and scratches, dinged by the preparation of thousands of meals. Vee had already set out placemats, china teacups, and small plates ringed with a delicate design of pink roses. A plate of ginger scones, smelling of sugar and spice, sat in the center. Genevieve was in the far corner of the room, talking in a low voice on her cell phone.

Vee poured the tea as her sister Fee bustled into the room, followed as always by her Scottish terrier. Mackie had arrived in the household over the fall and was a good deal livelier and less well behaved than his immediate predecessor. It must be hard for a dog to live in a B&B, a place that not only tolerated, but welcomed complete strangers every day. How was the poor thing to sort out who was invited and who was a threat? He sniffed around my workboots and the hems of my jeans. "Mackie, enough!" Fee commanded.

Genevieve finished her conversation and sat with us. Her alabaster skin was even paler than usual, her eyes deeply circled.

"Are you all right, my dear?" Fee placed a plump hand on top of Genevieve's. "I'm sure your employer's death has been quite a shock."

"They're saying it's something he ate." Genevieve's brown eyes opened wide. "What if it was something I made that killed him?"

"There, there," Vee said. "I'm sure it wasn't."

"But I left his food, his lunch and his dinner, all plated and ready to be served. What else could it have been?"

I'd seen the dinner. Cold lobster surrounding the lobster body that clutched the ring. Caviar in a silver bowl sitting in ice. Salmon, toast points, and cold asparagus. Strawberries dipped in chocolate. Very elegant. It didn't look like it had been touched. "What did you leave for Geoffrey's lunch?" I asked.

"A curried chicken salad he particularly liked. It's made with celery and water chestnuts, so it has a real crunch to it. And a loaf of crusty bread. Mr. Bower loved good bread."

"Has Maria Consuelo turned up? She's Genevieve's cabinmate," I explained to Fee and Vee. "The police couldn't reach her last night."

"I just got off the phone with Rick, the steward," Genevieve answered. "She didn't return to the ship this morning. I'm so worried about her. She's young. Only nineteen. I should have looked out for her.

Made sure she had something to do yesterday. I should have talked the other crew members into taking her with them." Genevieve's teacup was still full. Her scone sat on the plate, untasted. "Maybe I should have brought her here."

"I don't think Tom would have liked that," Fee said softly.

Genevieve's eyes brimmed with tears. "I was only thinking of myself, my weekend. I should've realized . . . she's a teenager."

"Genevieve." I said her name more sharply than I meant to. "You are not responsible for her. If anyone, it should have been Rick, her boss, who looked out for her."

"If anything has happened to her—"

"Maybe nothing has. Maybe she was perfectly capable of looking after herself and is late returning to the boat."

"You're right. I'm letting my imagination run away with me." She fell silent. A tear leaked out of her eye and snaked down her cheek. She brushed it away with her palm.

Vee took a last sip from her cup. "I'm so sorry this has happened to you, Genevieve."

"Thank you," Genevieve replied. "It's wonderful being here at the Snuggles where you take such good care of me. And to have Tom here with me too. I just feel . . ." She hesitated, cradling her head in her hands. "I feel I should be over at Blount's, with my crew family."

A look passed between Fee and Vee, around Genevieve's bowed head. "You haven't been with them all that long," Fee finally said. "Only a few months." I understood she wasn't trying to diminish Genevieve's ties to the crew. She was trying to build up Flynn. He'd been in Genevieve's life a lot longer than the workers on the *Garbo*.

"You were the newest of the crew," I pointed out. I too was on Team Flynn.

Genevieve pulled her head up. "The captain joined the same time I did. We picked him up in Sardinia as well."

"Two new crew members? Seems like a lot of turnover. Was Mr. Bower difficult to work for?" I asked.

"He was a sweetheart. Easy to please, grateful. All he asked was that wherever we were, the food be fresh and local. Emil, Doug, and Rick have been with Mr. Bower forever, but the rest of us were new. Ian and Maria Consuelo joined a few months before I did. Turnover isn't unusual on yachts. It's an isolated life. Lots of people think it would be a fun way to live, but after a year or two on board they get homesick and go back to working on dry land. The captains are about the only ones who can't do that. There's no equivalent job for them."

"So there's less change among captains?"

"Yes and no. They're ambitious like everyone else. There's always a more beautiful boat, a more prestigious owner. In the *Garbo*'s case, though, I understand Mr. Bower let the previous captain go. With the refit coming up, he wanted someone new."

I finished my tea and the last delicious bite of my scone. It contained tiny chunks of candied ginger that made my tongue tingle. "Thank you so much," I said to the sisters. "I have to get going."

"The clambake opens in five days," Fee sang out. "I can't wait for Family Day."

"You're all coming," I said. "Genevieve, you too, if you're still in town. Can you walk me out?"

Once the kitchen door had swung closed behind us, I leaned toward her. "Did Geoffrey ask you to put anything in the lobster's claw when you plated the salads?"

"Lobster's claw? He was specific that he wanted lobster, with a body for decoration, like a center-piece, but he didn't say anything about the lobster's claw."

"Did you think he wanted everyone off the *Garbo* because he was going to ask Wyatt to marry him?"

"What? No!" She grinned, the first smile I'd seen from her since she'd been summoned back to Blount's the night before. "I assumed, we all assumed, Mr. Bower was planning a seduction."

"A seduction?" We were at the front screen door. I turned to her.

"Ms. Jayne had her own cabin. She didn't stay in Mr. Bower's quarters. The general gossip around the *Garbo* was that last night was to be *the* night."

Chapter 13

"Quentin asked me to help Wyatt out with this investigation," I told Livvie and Sonny.

We were in the tiny clambake kitchen on Morrow Island. Livvie moved around the cramped space with a sure familiarity, pulling out the big pots used for the clam chowder, the baking pans used for the blueberry grunt dessert, and the saucepans used to melt butter for the lobster. Everything had to be scrubbed. I wiped the pantry shelves, getting them ready for the flour, sugar, crackers, and paper goods that would be stored there. Sonny washed down the commercial refrigerator and freezer. Baby Jack slept in a swing in the doorway.

We danced around, each one trying not to get in the others' way. It was hard to believe Livvie and three additional cooks put out food for two hundred people in the cramped space.

"What does that mean?" The big pot Livvie bent over amplified her voice with a tinny echo.

"It means he thinks Wyatt's gonna be suspect number one," Sonny answered.

Livvie looked at me, and I nodded. "Yes, that certainly seems possible."

Sonny grunted. "Seems to me it will be hard for you to help her, given you don't like her."

"I never said I didn't like her."

"This is why you're a lousy poker player." Sonny crossed his arms over his big chest. "You're easier to read than a book."

I stepped away from the shelves and stood upright. "Really? What have I ever said about her?"

"It's not what you say, it's what you do," Livvie answered. "Mom says whenever Wyatt's around, you're wound up so tight Mom's afraid you're going to explode. What did she ever do to you?"

I rinsed my sponge out in the deep sink and didn't answer.

Sonny took off to do some work around the island. Jack woke up and gently complained from his swing. I picked him up. He was a solid, muscular little dude, able to hold his head up from day one, and now sitting up and rolling over with ease. I jiggled him in my arms. I'd missed this early time with Page, when I'd been off in Manhattan. I was savoring it with Jack.

Livvie pulled her head out of the oven and adjusted her rubber gloves. "You know you have to help Wyatt, right?" she said. "Julia, it's Quentin."

I grunted an acknowledgment and changed the subject. "Tell me what you know about Vanessa. And her mother, Emmy. What's her deal?"

From across the little room, Livvie raised an eyebrow at me. "Why do you ask?"

"Just interested."

"I don't know a lot. Now that Page is in fifth grade, I know less about her friendships than I did back in the days of playdates." Livvie stuck her head back in the oven, so I had to strain to hear. She'd only taken charge of the kitchen the previous year. Before that, she'd worked at our ticket kiosk on the pier in order to stay in the harbor, to be on hand in case Page needed her. But the fire at Windsholme and related tragedies had caused a lot of changes. Sonny had taken over as our bake master, Livvie helmed the kitchen, and they had moved for the summer to the little house next to the dock. They would move out for this season shortly after school ended on Monday. My mother objected. She thought Jack was too small to live a boat ride from town and doctors, but Livvie was determined. Mom, after all, had spent every summer on the island until my dad had died, including the summers when Livvie and I were infants.

"All I can tell you is they moved here this winter into a trailer on Emmy's grandmother's property. But then you saw it, when you drove Vanessa home this morning. When Vanessa started school after the Christmas break, she and Page took to each other right away. She's different than Page's other friends from the swim team. Those two are closer somehow."

"And Emmy works at Crowley's."

"As many hours as she can. I don't think she was able to find anything over the winter when Crowley's was closed. I took Vanessa back to the trailer a few cold nights and wanted to turn around and take her back home with me. It was freezing in that place. It has heat, but I think Emmy kept it real low to save money and the windows leaked so much cold air the curtains were blowing."

Livvie finished in the oven, stood up, and closed its door with a satisfied *thunk*. "You noticed the green eyes."

"Yes."

"If you're worried about what they mean, ask Chris."

"Just like that? Do I say, 'Chris, I notice this kid has the same coloring as you. Anything you'd like to tell me?'"

Livvie laughed. "I'm sure you can do better than that. But yes, more or less. Ask him directly. That's what grown-up couples do."

It was my turn to laugh. I still couldn't get over how life had turned us upside down. My baby sister, the rebel, the wild one, was now the person who gave me the wisest advice. "I'm not that worried. Chris and Emmy seem to barely know each other."

"Ask him."

Jack wiggled and whined in my arms. "He must be wet," Livvie said.

I scooped up his diaper bag. "I'll take care of it."

I put Jack's changing pad on the counter in the gift shop and laid him down. Keeping one hand on his tummy to hold him steady, I fished in the bag for diapers and wipes. I smiled down at Jack and he smiled back at me. He was still bald, with only the tiniest wisps of blond hair. Page had been a surprise, conceived while Livvie was a senior in high school, before her parents were married or even engaged. But the worst thing that had happened in our little family to that point turned out to be the best thing, as baby Page kept us together as a family in the year of my father's illness and after his death. Jack, on the other hand, had been longed for and looked for, arriving ten years after his sister, and five years after Livvie had miscarried. I'd gotten pretty good at the diapering, something I never mastered when Page was an infant.

As I worked, my mind traveled back to prep school and to Wyatt and her friends.

The two weeks before the luncheon for Ms. Davis were a frenzy of planning and activities. The girls often met in our room checking things off our to-do list. First, Wyatt invited Ms. Davis. We held our collective breath until we agreed on a date when she was free and her husband, who coached soccer and was often tied up on Saturdays, could babysit. Then Lainey made the reservation at the inn, the most elegant eating establishment in town. It was an old boutique hotel that accommodated tourists in foliage season and the parents of the wealthiest students when they came for parents' weekends and graduations. Those important details out of the way, the conversation turned to what we would talk about and what we would wear.

During the discussions of appropriate luncheon topics, I tried to steer the conversation toward the literary. The girls were polite, adding questions about her favorite books as a child and current best sellers to the list. We also added politics and travel. We all wanted to appear grown up, worthy of her conversation. Lainey insisted on a discussion about fashion. It was a nonstarter in my opinion. Ms. Davis had dressed all fall in sweater sets over simple A-line wool skirts, but I wasn't willing to argue too hard and the topic was approved by the group.

When it came to what to wear, I had some considerations the others did not. Though the clothes I'd brought to school were perfectly fine, some gifts from my parents and family, some bought with the tips I earned at the clambake, none of them had labels of the type the other girls were discussing. Alone in my room, I tried on every dress I owned and finally settled on a long-sleeved navy blue one, which I hoped was generic enough not to draw attention or comment. Then there was the cost of a meal. My parents had given me an allowance and I still had some summer money, but I didn't have a credit card tied to a parental account like the other girls. I spent many anxious minutes scanning the inn's menu online, doing math in my head figuring how much cash I would need to bring to cover my meal, my contribution to Ms. Davis's meal, and the tip.

Despite that, I was happy to be included. At home, in elementary and middle school, I'd always felt like an outsider. My parents' strange marriage between a townie and a summer person left me in neither one camp nor the other. I hadn't expected to be accepted in prep school, much less by a group like Wyatt's.

"JULE-YA! Let's go!" Sonny stuck his head in

the gift shop. "Livvie's nearly done. Time for us to head back."

Sonny took Jack from me and carried him away toward the Boston Whaler. Livvie and I stood on the lawn, looking up at Windsholme. The sun was low enough in the western sky that it glinted off the remaining windows.

"We didn't finish our meeting last night," I said.

Livvie didn't waver. "Mom wants to rebuild, Julia. I don't see what there is to discuss."

I thought about Geoffrey Bower and the protesters. "Do you think that's the right thing to do, to fix up an extravagant mansion no one will ever live in, at least not full time, when Vanessa and her mother can't even heat their trailer in the winter?"

Livvie made no reply, so I continued. "Vanessa is worried if we tear down Windsholme, the ghost of Randy Brownly won't know where to find the ghost of Lenora Bailey."

"Then rebuild it we must," Livvie replied.

Chapter 14

We split up as soon as we got to town. Livvie and her family walked back to Mom's house so they could pick up her minivan. I headed across the footbridge toward Blount's. I called Wyatt as I walked, so she was waiting for me in the lobby.

"Thank you for coming. Quentin said he'd asked you to help me." Wyatt's shoulders were slumped, her brown hair dull and uncombed. The glamorous, vigorous Wyatt Jayne I'd encountered on Morrow Island two days before had been erased.

I led her out to the hotel patio. It was the end of the day, the cocktail hour. I asked the hostess for a table on the edge of the space, as far from the crowd at the outdoor bar as I could get us, and ordered two glasses of white wine. "I know Lieutenant Binder pretty well and Quentin thought I could be helpful," I explained when we were finally alone.

"Thank you!" Wyatt shocked me by throwing her arms around my neck and hugging me tight.

I disengaged, sitting back to look into her eyes.

"I didn't tell him yes." Tears came to her eyes again, threatening to spill over. She looked so forlorn. I felt terrible. "I didn't tell him no either. There are a couple of things I need you to be honest about before I put my reputation with these guys on the line."

She nodded her understanding. "Ask me anything."

"How do you know Quentin?"

It wasn't the question she'd expected. "We're old friends. I told you."

Exactly the answer he had given. "When did you meet?"

"In New York, the summer after I finished my undergrad."

"Did you work on his house?"

"His house here? I was a part of that team, though a junior one at the time. But that was a few years after I met him. Why are you asking about Quentin?"

Because I wanted to know why he felt obligated to her. Clearly she was more to him than an architect he was recommending to my mother. "Quentin said you were interviewed by the police again this morning."

"It was awful. I'm afraid they think I killed Geoffrey. They won't tell me what's going on. Not even exactly how he died, or why his face looked like that." She sat hunched over, arms tight across her chest. "Don't they always suspect the girlfriend? Do you think I need a lawyer if they talk to me again?"

"I have a friend, a local criminal lawyer who's

been helpful to me. Quentin knows him too. I can give you his name and number if you like."

"I didn't do it, Julia. Whatever it was that was done to him. Do they even know?"

I thought back to my conversation with Flynn that morning. "Last I heard, they hadn't determined exactly what killed him, but they believe it was something he ate or drank. Those tests will take a couple more days." The waitress delivered our wine and hurried off. "I'm sorry, Wyatt. I know this is hard for you. How did you and Geoffrey meet?"

"When he decided to refit the *Garbo* at the boat-yard here, he hired my firm to design the interiors. I was assigned to the job."

"How long ago was this?"

"Eight months."

I counted backward. October. "And your work assignment developed into a romance."

"Not right away. We worked together closely. I've never had such a strong, shared vision with a client. We were effortlessly in sync. It moved me."

The drawings she'd showed us of the refit of the *Garbo* were certainly beautiful, and harmonious, the product of a successful collaboration.

"How did you work together, logistically?"

"He was already in the Mediterranean. The typical pattern was we'd talk on the phone about what he wanted for each deck. I'd draw up plans and e-mail them to him. He'd come back with comments and changes. Occasionally, if we had to look at something together, we'd videoconference. We had a lovely working relationship."

"And then it got more personal."

"Yes, gradually it crossed that line. His e-mails to me were warm and friendly from the beginning. As time went on they became more personal." She sighed. "He wrote the most beautiful things. He sent flowers and gifts to my office. We'd talk on the phone all night. It was so old-fashioned and romantic. Not like guys our age."

"Did you ever meet Geoffrey in person? I mean before the *Garbo* came to Busman's Harbor?"

"Yes, twice. We met once in the beginning of the design process, in Portofino, before our relationship changed, and once more toward the middle, in Capri. You can't imagine settings more conducive to falling in love." Wyatt sat up a little straighter and even managed a fleeting smile.

"When you met, did anything about him strike you as odd?"

"You mean that he was a billionaire who never left his yacht? Of course it was odd. I'm not an imbecile, Julia." The mood in our little corner of the patio changed quickly. Color rose in her face and her voice took on the hard, dismissive edge I'd known so well at school. I braced for her to come after me with both barrels, but instead she slumped, the wind gone out of her. "I wish you had gotten to know him better. He was the most charming gentleman."

"Geoffrey toured those places with you? Portofino, Capri?" I coaxed.

"No. He never left the *Garbo*. At Capri, we took the launch around the island at sunset. It was beautiful, but we never went ashore. He was worried about his security. And there were always the protesters."

"He drew protesters everywhere? Even in Europe?"

"Europe had a banking crisis too," she reminded me. "That's why he wanted the *Garbo* to fit his taste so perfectly, because it was his home."

Sounds more like a prison. "Had you talked about the future?" Had she intended to live aboard the redone yacht, roaming the earth, never disembarking? Couldn't imagine a life like that. So glamorous on the outside, so hollow and disconnected on the inside.

Her face fell. "We hadn't gotten as far as discussing the future. And now we never will. It feels like it was a dream. I woke up this morning wondering if it had ever happened—the boat, Capri, the murder. Today, when that Lieutenant Binder questioned me, I had to keep repeating in my head, 'This is real. This is real. This is real.'" She broke down, sobbing noisily. I reached across the table and held her hand. I didn't like her. I had never liked her. But nobody deserved this.

Wyatt may have thought the future was a long way off, but it seemed like Geoffrey had planned for it to arrive sooner. "Wyatt, were you expecting Geoffrey to propose to you last night?"

She sat up straight, pulling her hand away as she did. "You're asking about the diamond you supposedly saw last night. The lieutenant asked me

about it. I swear I didn't see it and I didn't expect it.
I expected . . ." Wyatt took a deep breath. "I expected
he wanted to sleep with me."

Her shock seemed genuine. Unless she was an
award-worthy actress, she'd had no idea Geoffrey
was about to propose. And she hadn't noticed the
ring on the table.

I walked Wyatt back to her room. I offered to stay,
but she said she wanted to be alone.

My stomach rumbled. I decided to grab a burger
at Crowley's. On the way, I passed Busman's Harbor's
ugly, modern town-hall-police-station-firehouse. A
familiar state police sedan sat in the parking lot. I
walked through the door on the police side and approached the civilian dispatcher. "Lieutenant Binder
in?" I cocked my head toward the closed door to the
multipurpose room that the state police used when
they were in town.

"I'll check if he's free." She spoke into her head-
set, nodding as she did. "You can go in."

Lieutenant Binder looked up from his laptop.
Under his ski-slope nose, his mouth opened into a
genuine grin. At least it felt genuine. "Julia Snowden. To what do I owe the honor? We don't have an
appointment, do we?"

"No, no appointment. Just a deep curiosity." I sat
in the folding chair on the other side of his folding
table. He hadn't asked me to, I just did. I hoped the

act sent a signal I intended to stay, and had every right to be there.

If me sitting down bothered Binder, he didn't show it. "Not much I can tell you, yet. We'll be briefing the press on the results of the autopsy tomorrow."

"But you have some preliminary results."

"I do. And I don't see any harm in telling you. Geoffrey Bower was poisoned by something he ingested. His stomach contents are still being analyzed, but most likely it was something he ate." He paused, looking at me. "You don't have to pretend to look surprised. I know Sergeant Flynn told you."

Flynn was off the case, but the two of them were clearly communicating. "Was the 'something he ate' on that dining table at the time of his death?"

"We're testing everything, as you might assume, but no. He'd been dead for several hours when Ms. Jayne found him at eight o'clock. Nothing from that meal was found in his stomach contents. The medical examiner doesn't know exactly what the poison was, but from that awful look on his face, the thinking is it's something that causes seizures. The perimortem bruising on his body supports that conclusion. He would have been a mess—on the floor, clothes disheveled, drooling or worse. It's likely the entire scene you saw was staged after his death."

"Who would do that? And why?" This was new information. If the scene was staged, an enormous amount of work was put into the tableau.

Binder didn't have to look in his notes to find the

answer. "According to the forensic psychologist who consults with the department, the scene-setting shows regret, a desire to put things back as they were before the crime was committed. It means there was a deep connection between the killer and the victim."

"And everyone from the crew had left before he died?" I asked.

Binder pulled something up on the laptop and scanned, squinting. "Allegedly."

"Are there security cameras on the dock or on the *Garbo*?"

"No."

"The hotel I get," I said. "None of the hotels around here have security cameras. They're small and informal, even Blount's. But no cameras on a yacht that size with a full-time bodyguard on board? That seems odd."

"Maybe. But as we know, Bower valued his privacy." His cell phone vibrated on the desk. He picked it up, "Hang on a minute." Turning back to me he said, "Excuse me I have to take this."

I stood. "Of course, of course. Has Maria Consuelo turned up yet?"

He muted the phone with a flick of his thumb. "No sign of Ms. Lopez"

I hesitated. "And the diamond?"

"The diamond that Ms. Jayne didn't see and Mr. Durand didn't see? The diamond that only you saw?"

"Are. You. Looking for. It?" I said the words clearly and distinctly.

"Julia, I've had officers and crime scene techs

swarming all over that boat all day. You see what an enormous job it is. That ship has more nooks and crannies than an English muffin." He gave me one final stare. "We've put out the word to pawn shops from here to Boston. I'm taking it seriously. That's all I can tell you. I really have to take this call."

And with that, I was dismissed.

Chris was working the door when I arrived at Crowley's. Though he mumbled hello and bent to give me a hug, he kept his eyes on the sidewalk. The Crowley's building was an old harborside ware-house, the kind of place with high ceilings and rough wooden floors. The drinks were expensive and watered down. The locals avoided it, except for a small group of "family," the spouses, boyfriends, and girlfriends of the employees, and of whichever band was playing that evening. I made my way to their usual table.

The band was on a break and there wasn't a seat at the long table for me. When the chef's husband started to get up, I put out my hand. "I'm here for a meal. I'll grab a seat at the bar."

"Don't be silly, we'll pull a chair over." He re-trieved one for me from a nearby table.

I ordered my burger—cheese, cooked onion, medium rare—and we caught up on the events of the winter and spring. It was a mixed crew, includ-ing several people I wouldn't have normally been friends with, but sitting at that table had a cool, insider vibe, one I'd rarely experienced in my life, a vibe I reveled in.

It didn't take long for the conversation to turn to the murder on the mega-yacht. The theories abounded, everything from suicide to the Russian mafia. "He was a billionaire who made money on the banking collapse. Of course he was a target," someone said.

"It was the girlfriend," the husband of the chef declared.

"Why do you say that?" I kept my tone conversational, not challenging.

"It's always the girlfriend," he answered.

"I don't see how it benefits her," I countered.

"Maybe he was terrible in bed," someone offered.

"If that were a reason for murder, half the men at this table would be dead," the bartender's wife joked.

"What do you mean, half?" a girlfriend of one of the band members deadpanned. Everybody laughed.

"Maybe he was a jerk."

Maybe he had been—though the man I'd met had seemed quirkily charming, neither an eccentric recluse nor a cartoonishly villainous financier. Quentin had asked me if I thought Wyatt was capable of murder. When my imagination allowed me to consider she might be, I didn't think she was the type to murder a jerky boyfriend in a fit of anger. Besides, poison required premeditation. Staging a death scene required postmeditation. Geoffrey Bower's murder hadn't been a crime of passion.

The waitress delivered my burger and I dug in.

Delicious and cooked to perfection. The best place to order bar food was in a bar.

"What about his chef, the Pelletier woman?" the bartender's wife asked. "She was a suspect in a murder in town last fall."

"She wasn't guilty," someone else pointed out. "She wasn't even involved."

"Yeah, but she's been murder *adjacent*. Makes me wonder."

With that remark, all eyes turned toward me. I was the most murder-adjacent person at the table by a wide margin. "What do you think, Julia?"

"I know Wyatt Jane and Genevieve Pelletier. I can't picture either of them committing murder."

The band members slowly got up from the table and returned to the slightly raised platform that served as a stage. Once gathered, they started up a raucous number. Couples rose to dance. From across the room, Emmy Bailey spotted me and waved with her free hand. The other held a tray filled with beer bottles. I waved back.

"What do you know about the new waitress?" I shouted over the music.

"I hear she's nice," the bartender's wife said. "A hard worker."

"I think she has a kid," the chef's husband added.

"Two," I shouted back. "The ten-year-old is a friend of my niece." I wondered who was caring for Vanessa while Emmy worked tonight. My mom or my sister was my guess. "Do you know where they're from?"

"Moved here this winter from Phippsburg," the woman on my right answered. "I think Emmy grew up in Bath, but there's a local connection. Her grandparents lived out on Thistle Island. Her grandma's still there. That's why Emmy moved here."

A town connection, especially a long established one, elevated one's standing with the locals. It was working to Emmy's benefit with this crowd.

"What's with the interest?" the chef's husband asked. "Chris was over here earlier tonight asking the exact same questions."

That shut me up. I pushed my plate away, half the burger still on it, and scanned the room. Chris was at his usual station by the door. Why had he been asking about Emmy?

As I watched, Quentin came in, shook Chris's hand, and leaned in to ask him something. Chris nodded yes and pointed in my direction. It was only then that I thought to check my phone, which was in my tote bag, hanging on the back of my chair. But there were no recent texts or calls. Whatever Quentin wanted, it couldn't be too urgent if he'd come looking for me instead of calling. I said my good-byes and left money on the table to cover my meal.

"Take a walk?" Quentin asked.

"Sure." I turned to ask Chris if he planned to sleep at the apartment, but he'd moved rapidly toward the dance floor where a drunk young man stood, screaming obscenities at his equally drunk partner. I followed Quentin out the door.

"Wyatt told me you talked to her." Quentin was

beside me as we walked toward my apartment. His step was jaunty, his arms swung loosely at his sides. "Does this mean you're going to help?"

I didn't answer the question directly. "I've spoken to Tom Flynn, Lieutenant Binder, Genevieve Pelletier, and Wyatt. I'm interested in following this case. I'll pass anything I hear that's of value along to you and to Wyatt."

Quentin nodded. "I hear you. I can't ask for more."

"I don't think you have much to worry about," I assured him. "Why would Wyatt kill her super-rich boyfriend? What's her motive? Unless the police have something we don't know about, they'll move on from her soon." I stopped on the sidewalk, turning to face him. "Normally, anything that included the police, reporters, and crime would have you running in the other direction."

"I do value my privacy."

"So what's different about this situation? Why are you running toward it?"

He started off again. I did a quickstep to stay by his side. "I'm not running toward it." His voice was forceful in denial. "But I care about Wyatt."

"Why do you care so much about Wyatt?"

"I've told you. She's an old friend. You would do the same for a friend. Have done, in fact."

I stopped again. "You don't have friends."

He took a step back. "That's mean. I thought we were friends."

We'd been over this ground before. The asymmetrical nature of our relationship. Where he knew everything about my family and me and was comfortable commenting about it. Where I knew next to nothing about him. We'd left it hanging the previous fall when he'd taken off for warmer climates. Here we were again. He looked startled and a little hurt. I didn't want to hurt him, but I didn't want to offer any reassurances either. I wanted him to tell me the truth.

Chapter 15

I awoke the next morning, alone in my bed. There was a text from Chris. SLEEPING ON THE DARK LADY. It had come in long after I'd gone to sleep, after Crowley's closing time, after he'd driven the last drunk home in the cab he owned, his third job. I lay for a moment in my cozy bed, nostalgic for the winter, when we'd run the restaurant and lived together every day.

From downstairs came the sounds of chattering and cooking for the early crowd at Gus's. There would be a lull, then the post-church crew would arrive. Though I wouldn't have believed it if someone had told me a year ago, I loved living in a place with rhythms and seasons I knew so well.

I pushed the sheet and summer blanket aside and put my feet on the floor. Outside the big window, the sky was gray and streaks of water ran down the glass. A rainy day, as expected. Tourists from New England and New York would probably head home early, depriving the local restaurants of lunch trade, the minigolf courses and boat tours of customers. I felt lucky we were unaffected, our opening still a few days away. Captain George, the pilot of our tour boat, planned a shakedown cruise for the afternoon. He'd already trained his crew, mostly new hires, in how to work the lines, work behind the snack bar, and keep the guests safe. Today he'd take them to the island and back. It would burn a lot of fuel with no return, but seeing how they performed underway, and doing any last-minute training, would be invaluable. I hoped to join the boat when it sailed at noon.

In the meantime, I had a rare morning to myself. I pulled on my clothes, ducked out Gus's back door, and headed for Blount's.

On the footbridge, I paused to look toward the *Garbo*. The rain had stopped, though the sky was still gray. I closed my umbrella and stowed it in my tote. The yacht sat in the calm harbor, dignified and imposing, despite the yellow crime scene tape that crisscrossed the dock. All was quiet on the yacht, but there were two small boats next to her in the water. One belonged to the state police and one to the Maine Marine Patrol. A man in black scuba gear pushed himself off the state police boat backward, joining at least two others who were in the water. What were they looking for? The diamond? Or the body of Maria Consuelo? Was she still missing? I hugged my arms tight to my sides and resumed walking.

Who owned the *Garbo* now? There would be

probate and all that stuff, no doubt complicated for someone as rich as Geoffrey. But who had inherited that magnificent ship? Would whoever it was go through with the refit? Probably not on schedule. There would be layoffs at Herndon's if the job was pulled at the last minute.

When I got to Blount's, I had the kid at reception call Emil Nicolescu's room. I was surprised when the bodyguard agreed to take my call, and even more surprised when he said he'd meet me in the hotel coffee shop.

"I'm here. What do you want?" His English was fluent, his accent subtle, like he'd learned the language when he was young, before his palate hardened and the way he used his tongue became uncontrollable habit.

"Thank you for seeing me." We entered the coffee shop, where the hostess escorted us to a small table by the windows that looked out on the harbor, the dock, and the *Garbo*, crime scene tape and all.

He squinted at me warily from under thick, black eyebrows. "I do not think you have come to me to make chitchat. I understand you are a busy woman, with some sort of tourist attraction to open." He paused, hands on the table, steepling fingers as big as hot dogs. His knowledge about my connection to the Snowden Family Clambake, the "tourist attraction," as he called it, meant he had checked me out. Exactly who at this table was using whom to get information? "You are an old friend of Miss Jayne's," he finished.

The waitress arrived. Emil ordered a coffee,

"black, strong." I did the same. "With milk," I added. The pause in the conversation gave me a chance to consider my tactics. I made a decision. "Wyatt and I are old classmates, as you said. The police may consider her a suspect in Geoffrey's death. I want to help her out, if I can."

"You have aided the police in previous inquiries." He looked at me and nodded. "I have asked the Google."

"Yes, that's true. Look"—I spread my hands out on the table, miming showing my cards—"this situation can't be good for you. You were Geoffrey Bower's bodyguard, and he's been murdered. You want an explanation and I need an explanation. I'll tell you what I know, and you tell me what you know."

He nodded his agreement. "Fine. You go first."

The waitress arrived with our coffees in white ceramic mugs and a small pitcher of cream. She returned with bowls of sugar, loose and cubed, a vessel holding packets of sweetener. I would have expected nothing less of Blount's.

"Here's what I know," I started. "Two nights ago, Wyatt invited my friend, my boyfriend, and me to dinner aboard the *Garbo*."

"Seems—what you say? Presumptuous," he said. "It is not her ship to invite people to."

"You tell me. Did Wyatt have the . . . I guess you would call it 'standing' as Geoffrey's girlfriend to invite friends to dinner?"

"I would not have said so, no. Mr. Bower never had guests, never. He forbid the crew to have guests as well. And Wyatt has only been a guest on the yacht three times."

"That would be when she visited at Portofino, at Capri, and this week."

He nodded. "She has been staying on the yacht all week. But this, we were told, was for her work, at her insistence. So she could see how Mr. Bower lived aboard and what he needed, for any last-minute additions to the furniture or equipment for the refit." He looked down at the table. "She stayed in her own quarters."

The same thing Genevieve had indicated. Wyatt had implied it as well. She wasn't sleeping with Geoffrey. "She didn't stay in Mr. Bower's quarters?"

"Most definitely not. When people move around the yacht at night, it is my job to know this."

"You're on duty day and night?" When did he sleep?

"No, no. Normally I have a team of three or four working for me, but while we are here for the fixing of the yacht, the crew are skeletons."

"A skeleton crew," I confirmed.

"Yes, this."

"What time did you leave the *Garbo* on Friday?" I asked.

"Just after two PM. Mr. Bower had asked for privacy. I waited while Rick set the dining room table for two. The captain and I helped him move the food from the refrigerator in the galley, where Chef Genevieve left it, to the small one in the service area off the dining room. He put luncheon out for Mr. Bower. Then Rick, Marius, and I left the boat."

"And you were gone the rest of the day."

"Rick went along to the beach. This is his favorite preoccupation. Captain Marius and I thought we would enjoy being tourists in Portland. We arrived back when you saw in this hotel that night."

On a long June evening, the restaurants and bars of the Old Port in Portland would be teeming with people. I imagined Emil, of the broad shoulders, and Captain Marius, of the flowing brown hair, creating quite a stir, particularly if they casually mentioned they were in Maine on a mega-yacht. People would remember them. Women would remember them. I assumed the state police had checked their statements. I'd try to pry the information out of Binder later.

"Who was still on the boat when you left?"

"All had left. Part of my job was to be the last one off."

"It's a big boat. How could you be sure?"

"I inspected it, of course. There was no one aboard but Mr. Bower, Rick, and Marius, who left with me. But more important, I saw them all leave. Chef Genevieve left with her boyfriend first. Ian and Doug left together when they finished their morning tasks, around noon."

"What about Wyatt? She wasn't part of the crew."

"Miss Jayne had left earlier. Around eleven thirty. Her leaving the boat, and then returning for dinner was necessary to Mr. Bower's surprise for her."

"And Maria Consuelo?" As far as I knew the young stewardess still wasn't accounted for.

"I did not see her leave," Emil admitted. "But I had inspected the boat, including her cabin, the galley, the crew room. I am confident she was not on board."

"Was it difficult to provide security for Geoffrey?" Apart from the whole being murdered thing, Geoffrey seemed like an ideal client. He never left the ship. And he wasn't a big celebrity. But there had been the protesters, which seemed weird for an obscure billionaire.

Emil threw his hands in the air. "The hate. The hate. You do not understand the hate directed at this man."

"No, I don't understand it." I really didn't. "I get that he was rich, but what did he do?"

"This, truly, I do not understand. It was my job to read the e-mails. They come every day, sometimes nearly a hundred. They accuse him of everything bad that has happened in their lives. The loss of their homes, health, jobs, loved ones."

"Did you pass these threats on to Geoffrey?"

"No. I have strict instructions not to tell him. When I thought the threats were real, I forwarded them to a special e-mail box to keep them secure. Then I would increase security on the yacht. Advise the captain to stay at sea, avoid the ports. Have a crew member stand watch all through the night."

"Who gave you these instructions?"

"Mr. Bower himself did."

"Did he ever give any indication he went into the special mailbox and read the e-mails?"

"No. Never."

Perhaps Geoffrey didn't want to know. The hate mail had pushed him out to sea, away from the rest of humanity. Why would he want the details? "Had there been any credible threats lately?"

"None. We are in this place." He looked out the coffee shop window at the part of the harbor that was visible around the gigantic *Garbo*. A family went out for a sail. A lobster boat chugged along, laden with traps destined for the harbor floor. "So peaceful. So hidden. I thought, when we arrived, 'Nothing bad can happen here.'" He let out a defeated sigh. "I was wrong."

"Did you tell Lieutenant Binder about the threats?"

"Yes. Reluctantly. Mr. Bower prefers his privacy, but this situation is unique. The police are reviewing the e-mails now."

"There's a safe in Geoffrey's office on the yacht," I said. "What's in it?"

"As far as I have known, I have only seen him use the safe for important papers, papers of great confidentiality."

"No jewelry?"

Emil considered, but not for long. "I do not think so. What need would a single man have for jewelry?"

"How long have you worked for Mr. Bower?"

"From the beginning, before he moved onto the *Garbo*. Eight years, almost to the day. Tomorrow would have been my anniversary." Up until then, the big bodyguard had been businesslike, gruff, but with the last sentence his voice broke. He seemed genuinely sad at the loss of his employer.

"And before you worked for Mr. Bower?" I asked.

"I did similar work for a famous person. A name you would recognize. I have signed a nondisclosure, so I could not tell you the name, even if I cared to. Which I do not." Emil motioned for the check.

"I'll get it," I said. I'd invited him. "I'd like to talk to the others."

"I can't stop you, if they agree. But you should know, every question you have asked, I have already answered."

"To Lieutenant Binder?"

"Yes, to him. And to Genevieve's boyfriend, this Flynn. I understand he is also a policeman."

So Flynn was making his own inquiries. *Fascinating*. But then, he was a man in love, whose girlfriend was worried she'd poisoned someone. Investigating was the obvious thing for a man like Flynn to do.

I walked with Emil to the lobby. As soon as he stepped into the elevator, I asked the receptionist to ring the captain. Emil and Marius had gone to Portland together, so I assumed they were friends. I needed to reach Marius before the bodyguard did. The receptionist nodded toward a house phone on the other side of the lobby. I made it there as the call rang through.

"Hello?"

"Captain Marius, this is Julia Snowden. We met the other night on the *Garbo*."

"Yes, yes, of course. And again in the conference room as we waited for our interrogations."

"I believe the detectives call them interviews."

"You are the attractive blonde." It was hard to imagine I'd been attractive that night, after seeing Bower's corpse. I pictured Captain Marius, the thick, wavy, brown hair that fell over one of his enormous brown eyes. I smelled a line. "Interviews. Interrogations. It makes no difference to me." He sounded casual, unconcerned.

"I'm in the lobby. I wonder if you would join me in the coffee shop. I'd like to ask you some questions about the *Garbo* and your work on the ship."

"Questions? Why would you ask the questions? I have already spoken to two policemen. Excuse me a moment. My mobile phone is ringing. Excuse."

Marcus's accent was stronger than Emil's and quite similar. Yacht captains, like airline pilots, were required to understand and speak English, as well as to have numerous licenses and certifications. The requirements only got more demanding as yachts went up in size, and the *Garbo* was enormous. So Marius definitely spoke English, but I wondered how much he understood of American lingo and culture, especially when the conversation wasn't about ships. Perhaps he had not understood that Flynn was asking him questions informally, not as a member of the police force.

"Hello?" Marius was back on the line. "I am sorry. I am called away. We will have this coffee another time." With a click, he was gone.

* * *

I hung up the house phone, nodded my thanks to the receptionist across the lobby, and went out the glass front door. On the walk, I ran smack into the leader of Thursday night's protest against Geoffrey Bower. The man who'd also been in the hotel lobby the night Geoffrey's body was removed. I recognized him instantly. He was memorably handsome, tall and lean with regular, masculine features. The kind of person anyone would give a second look to.

"Sorry." He stepped to the side.

"My fault," I answered. "I'm sorry. I'm Julia Snowden." I offered my hand and let it hang in the air until he had to respond.

"Cliff Munroe." He took my hand and shook it.

"Didn't I see you Thursday night on the dock beside the *Garbo*?"

He held up his hands, palms out. "Guilty as charged."

I laughed. "I'm not sure I'd throw that word around, given Geoffrey Bower's murder." The color rose behind his early-season tan. Protesting was outdoor work. The blush made him seem vulnerable, approachable. "Can we talk?" I asked.

"Sure. Here?" We were blocking the entrance to Blount's.

I pointed to Fishermen's Park next door. A statue and a flagpole sat on a little rise overlooking the harbor. The clouds had broken and the sky and sea offered up two different, dazzling shades of blue.

An American flag moved gently in the June sea breeze. There was a bench facing the sea.

The protester followed me and we sat, both of us staring at the water for a moment. On the other side of the harbor, the Snowden Family Clambake kiosk sat on the town pier, with our tour boat, the *Jacquie II*, anchored beside it. Captain George and his crew were already on board, carrying out preparations for their first cruise of the season. I'd have to hurry through the conversation if I wanted to make it.

"I know who you are," he said. "I've been following the investigation. As best as I can from a distance."

"Where are you from, Cliff?"

"New York City."

"Me too. Most recently North Moore Street. Tribeca. I live here now."

"Upper West Side."

That fit better with him than the idea of a scruffy protester. Though his hair had grown shaggy, he looked more Wall Street than Occupy Wall Street. "What brings someone like you all the way from the Upper West Side to protest against Geoffrey Bower?"

Munroe's eyes flashed. "The man's a monster. Do you know how he made his money?"

I thought back to my conversation with Quentin. "Something about the housing collapse?"

"He made billions betting against the housing market. While people suffered, lost their jobs, their homes, their futures, in some cases their lives."

"Wasn't that legal and, given what happened, smart?"

Munroe sat back on the bench. He had a backpack,

which he slipped off and pulled onto his lap. He opened it and handed me a pamphlet. In big black letters on the front it read, "GEOFFREY BOWER, ENEMY OF THE PEOPLE." "You tell me. Is it okay for him to live in luxury while so many people suffer? To profit off desperation and despair?" His voice rose as he came to the end of the sentence.

I knew about the desperation, and the despair. My family had almost lost our business, Morrow Island, our tour boat, and Mom's house to a terrible loan. I looked over at the *Garbo*. I didn't like the idea that Geoffrey Bower could enjoy that gleaming yacht while other people, elderly people, people with kids, lost everything. But had Geoffrey enjoyed it, or had he been a prisoner on it? And had people like Cliff Munroe, and the people who sent the threats Emil had told me about, made him so? "Your beef seems more personal than political," I said.

"It is," he said. "Deeply, deeply personal."

"How so?"

He ignored me, as if he hadn't heard the question, and sat staring out at the harbor. Three deep whistle blasts sounded. The ten-minute warning from the *Jacquie II*. I stood. "I have to run."

"Read the pamphlet I gave you," Munroe called after me, shouldering his backpack. "It's all in there. Then tell me what you think."

Chapter 16

I pelted down the pier as fast as my work boots would carry me and made it to the *Jacquie II* as the lines were released, hardly a good example for the young crew members on board. I ran up the stairs to the pilothouse, huffing and puffing. Captain George gave me a kindly look and steered the boat away from the dock.

"What do you want me to do?" I asked.

For as long as I could remember, Captain George had piloted the *Jacquie II*, bringing customers to Morrow Island. In July and August that would be two hundred people twice a day, back and forth, four total trips. The captain had been a friend of my father's and a friend to me as I'd struggled to keep the clambake afloat the previous season.

"Walk around and be a guest," he instructed. "Order from the snack bar. Ask questions. Inspect to make sure everything is clean and tidy. At some point, I'll run a safety drill."

George was one of the most experienced captains

in the harbor, but his crew was almost entirely new—a half dozen college students, only a few with boating experience. The jobs were excellent for kids who wanted to spend the summer outdoors, but the hourly pay was low and the tips sporadic. As a result, our waitstaff jobs were easier to fill. Unless employees were really committed to a life on boats, they almost always opted for a better-paying, island-based job if they returned for a second summer.

I left the bridge and walked down the center aisle that separated the seating on the open upper deck. The benches gleamed white in the sun, no dirt and no bird mess. Good job. On nice days most of our guests would sit up here, the better to experience the sights and sounds of the harbor.

Captain George began the tour narration with the mandatory safety announcement. Life vests for passengers on the top deck were in the gray bin behind the pilothouse. I went to it and opened the lid. Rows of neat, dry, orange vests sat inside, not tangled or otherwise compromised. Score another one for the crew.

Over the loudspeakers, Captain George continued speaking to our invisible guests, pointing out the hotels that lined both sides of the inner harbor, as well as the Lobster Deck, a restaurant that passed out our fliers in return for a plug. Soon we were away from the boats at their moorings and George began to speak about the history of Dinkum's Light, which lay straight ahead.

I climbed down to the main deck and ordered a draft beer from the snack bar. The young man in charge pulled the tap handle expertly and tilted the plastic cup to manage the foam. He was a cute kid, over twenty-one, since he was allowed to work the snack bar, but I didn't think by much. His khakis and navy blue polo shirt with the words "Snowden Family Clambake" stitched on the pocket made him look snappy. I asked the way to the ladies' room. He blushed slightly, but directed me to the passageway that led behind the snack bar.

The head was immaculate. Captain George had done a good job with the kids. The narration was piped into the bathrooms and I listened to his resonant voice as he pointed out seals sunning themselves, and osprey's and eagle's nests on little uninhabited islands of the outer harbor.

As I washed my hands his tone changed. "Fire. Fire in the snack bar." Captain George barked the words with authority, but without drama. A siren sounded. "Crew to your fire stations." Footsteps pounded across the deck above me. I ran to the main deck. A kid went charging by me toward the snack bar, a fire extinguisher over his head. He opened it expertly, and was about to douse the area, when I yelled, "Stop!"

I caught my breath. "Great job," I said to the crew members gathered around me "While he . . . what's your name?"

"Devon."

"While Devon put out the fire, what should the rest of you be doing?"

"Keeping the guests calm."

"Passing out life preservers."

"Readying the lifeboat for water evacuation."

"Readying the gangway in case of land evacuation."

A land evacuation is what Captain George would attempt in all but the direst situations. If the boat were navigable, he'd maneuver us to or near land. The water of the harbor was always deadly cold and especially so in June.

"Don't tell me, show me," I urged.

"Yes, ma'am!" They hurried to their respective stations.

"How'd that go?" Captain George asked when I returned to the pilothouse.

"You've trained them well. Glad we did it, though."

"You can only get so far on land. You have to drill. As long as they remember there's only one captain, and the captain's in charge, they'll be fine."

On Morrow Island, I directed the crew to unload the bags of onions and potatoes and stack them on the pantry shelves I had scrubbed the day before. Satisfied everything was shipshape, I headed down to the little house by the dock. Captain George had given his crew a break to blow off some steam. They'd retrieved a volleyball and net from our shed and were enjoying an energetic game.

Upstairs in the little house, I threw the small number of personal things I'd left there into a gym bag. Between one thing and another, I wasn't going to be sleeping on the island again. School ended the next day and Livvie and her family would move in soon after. I'd miss the quiet and the dark, dark nights with millions of stars.

Back downstairs, I sat at the dining table facing the picture window with a view of the Atlantic out to the horizon and opened the pamphlet Cliff Munroe had given me. It was a typical black-and-white, trifold design, the kind that could have been made at any copy shop.

The story it told was the same one the protester had outlined for me, but with a lot more exclamation marks.

THIS MAN PROFITS FROM YOUR PAIN!

While he sails in his gigantic motor yacht, you may have lost your home, your job, maybe even your health.

Geoffrey Bower made his $$$$$ betting against the US housing market. He bet against the big banks and the insurance companies. He bet you wouldn't be able to pay your mortgage, and in all too many cases, he was right.

He knew something was rotten, yet he said nothing. He didn't warn the regulators or the journalists or the pundits. He didn't try to warn you. He kept mum and made billions.

You live with the consequences of his actions. Maybe your house is still underwater. Maybe your retirement fund is depleted. Maybe you are still out of work or working part-time for low wages. Geoffrey Bower lives on in luxury!! But we must see to it he does not live in peace.

The pamphlet was signed "The Alliance for a Fairer Universe," which seemed like a grandiose and unachievable objective. Whoever they were, they had protested Geoffrey in Europe and in peaceful Busman's Harbor, hidden away at the eastern edge of the United States. It seemed odd. It seemed off. But I couldn't say how.

The *Jacquie II*'s whistle sounded, calling the crew back to their posts. I put the pamphlet in my tote bag and headed to the dock.

Chapter 17

As soon as we docked, I thanked Captain George and his crew and walked directly to the police station. I was surprised to find Lieutenant Binder behind his desk; he was a man who liked to take active part in his investigations, not a paperwork jockey. But perhaps without his faithful sergeant at his side, things were different.

"Ms. Snowden, I don't remember an appointment."

"We didn't have one."

"But nonetheless, you're hoping I'll update you on the investigation." He sat back in his desk chair.

"Can it really hurt?" He didn't answer, perhaps hoping his silence spoke for itself. "Tell you what," I continued. "What if I ask questions and you answer only the ones you're comfortable with?"

He laughed. "And what do I get in return?"

"I'll answer any question of yours. Not selectively. Anything."

"Go for it. How can I lose?" He folded his arms

across his chest, a gesture demonstrating the opposite of openness, despite his words.

I wiggled in the hard folding chair, hoping to get comfortable, but failing miserably. "Do you know more precisely what caused Geoffrey Bower's death?"

"We do." He put his glasses on, clicked on his screen, and then read, "Hemlock water dropwort. Botanical name: *Oenanthe crocata*, family: Umbelliferae." He stumbled over the Latin, as I certainly would have done.

"And what is that when it's at home?"

"It's a highly poisonous plant. Unusually, every part of it is poisonous—stem, flower, leaf, root."

"And how do you think it ended up in Geoffrey?"

"That is the question, now isn't it? For certain, he ate it."

"Was he force fed or did he eat it willingly?"

"From his stomach contents, it appears the plant was delivered in the curried chicken salad Genevieve says she made for his lunch. Unlike most poisonous plants, the hemlock water dropwort is quite tasty. The stems look like wild celery and the roots like parsnips. Poisoning of humans is rare, and almost always accidental—usually foragers and such." Binder shifted in his chair.

"Where does this dropwort stuff grow?"

"Everywhere. All over Europe and North America, including here in Maine. You've no doubt seen it. It grows in swampy areas, looks like a giant Queen Anne's lace."

"Could the poisoning have been an accident?

Something mislabeled that Genevieve bought at the farmer's market?"

"Highly doubtful. No one else in town is sick."

"Have you interviewed Genevieve since you received this information?"

"She's due here at any moment. When you came in, I thought you were her. Obviously, as the person who prepared Bower's food, she needs to be questioned."

How had the hemlock water dropwort gotten into the salad, assuming that is what happened? Had someone given it to Genevieve, who'd unknowingly prepared it? Or was it substituted later? I thought about Geoffrey's life, a man in exile. "Could he have poisoned himself?"

Binder looked up from his computer, squinting at me over the glasses. "You're suggesting that Bower purposefully ingested a poisonous plant, had several grand mal seizures and certainly vomited, cleaned himself up, dressed in that ridiculous yachting outfit, put all the dinner food out, and then sat behind his dining room table, before the last seizure carried him off, leaving a horrific tableau?"

I snorted a laugh. He was right. The scenario was ridiculous. "A horrific tableau for his girlfriend to discover," I added.

"Allegedly discover," he corrected.

"Is Wyatt Jayne still a person of interest?"

"We're expecting Mr. Bower's attorney tomorrow. He's been detained in New York by pressing interests related to Mr. Bower's business and his death, but he's provided us with Bower's most recent will and testament. You may be interested to learn that several years ago, after he made his fortune, Mr. Bower set up a foundation to build affordable housing to aid families who are homeless or in danger of becoming homeless."

"Ironic."

"Seems more like guilt to me," Binder said. "A week ago, Mr. Bower changed the trustee whom he designated to run the foundation in the event of his death."

"He named Wyatt," I guessed. *This isn't good.*

"He did. His attorney, Mr. Frederickson, was surprised and tried to talk his client out of making the change. Previously, Mr. Frederickson had been the trustee. He told me in conversation that he and Mr. Bower had been friends since childhood. Mr. Frederickson was under the impression he was Mr. Bower's only friend."

"Wyatt wouldn't have access to the money." I spoke my thought aloud. "Presumably, with that kind of funding, it would be a real charitable foundation with a board and oversight."

"No, she wouldn't have access to the funds for personal use," Binder agreed. "But according to Frederickson, it would catapult her to the top of a rarefied world where she'd have architectural and construction commissions to pass out like candy."

In other words, to the top of the world she already lived in. The Wyatt I knew was ambitious. "Does Wyatt know about this?"

"Mr. Frederickson informed her this morning. There's one strange, additional caveat to all of this.

Mr. Bower asked for Ms. Jayne to arrange his funeral. His parents are long gone and he has no children or siblings. The medical examiner is done with the remains. Ms. Jayne has arranged for his body to be shipped back here to Foreman's Funeral Home today."

"To Foreman's?" Given Geoffrey's wealth, I'd imagined a grand funeral in a New York cathedral. But then, who would have come?

"The funeral is to be here. And soon."

"He didn't know a soul here."

"I'm not sure he knew a soul anywhere. It appears, aside from Mr. Frederickson and Ms. Jayne, the crew members of the *Garbo* were the people closest to him. Ms. Jayne wants to hold the funeral before they scatter to the four corners of the earth."

Lieutenant Binder's information led inexorably in a circle. Binder had told me the police psychologist believed Geoffrey's body was staged by someone who felt remorse, someone who cared about him. With the exception of his lawyer, the people who cared about Geoffrey were all working or staying on the *Garbo*. Wyatt had motive, the others didn't. They had anti-motive, if that was a thing. They would lose their jobs. There had to be another motive Binder didn't know about.

What a sad life, to be mourned only by the people you employed. And how at odds it was with the smiling, charming man in the funny wig I'd met on Thursday night. "Have you found Maria Consuelo?" I finally asked.

"Ms. Lopez is still missing."

"Do you think she killed Geoffrey?"

Binder took off his reading glasses. "No. At least, not alone. Everyone has described her as a little slip of a thing. It would take enormous strength to dress Mr. Bower, lift him off the floor, and seat him at the table. My instinct is we're looking for two people, working together. We're searching everywhere for Ms. Lopez, but because we think she may have witnessed the crime or may even be another victim."

"You think two people killed Geoffrey?"

"I do. And a little too conveniently, the people of interest in this case break down into groups of two who alibi each other. Emil Nicolescu, the bodyguard, and Marius Alexandrescu, the captain, say they were together in Portland. And they were, at least in the evening. We've verified that with two bartenders in the Old Port. Ian Cowen, the deckhand, and Douglas Merriman, the engineer, were roaming bar to bar in Busman's Harbor. Again, we can account for part, but not all, of their time. Rick, the head steward, is the only one who seems to have spent time alone. He says he went to the beach before he met up with Mr. Cowen and Mr. Merriman, though we haven't found anyone to confirm it." He paused. "Genevieve Pelletier's alibi is, of course, provided by my own partner."

"You don't believe either of them had anything to do with this."

He hesitated before answering, but finally said, "No. I don't. Though Genevieve probably prepared the meal that killed him, so we have to look at her seriously."

"And Wyatt Jayne? Who's her alibi?"

Binder's head drew back, as if startled. "Why, Quentin Tupper, of course. She's said she was with him at his house on Westclaw Point all afternoon. I thought they would have told you that."

They hadn't told me. And given the lieutenant's theory the crime was committed by two people, that made Quentin a suspect too.

Chapter 18

The interview was interrupted by a knock at the door. The civilian receptionist informed Lieutenant Binder that Genevieve had arrived for their meeting. I rose, feeling like I'd gotten away with something. Binder had never gotten to question me, which was just as well, since I had some checking I wanted to do before I shared with him the information I thought I had. I passed Genevieve in the hall on my way out, gave her a quick hug, and wished her luck.

I called Quentin on the walk home, got no answer, and left a message on his voice mail that we needed to talk.

As I came up the harbor hill, I spotted Page and Vanessa sitting in the late afternoon sunshine on the floor of Mom's front porch, playing a messy card game of war. I was almost to the front steps when Page shouted, "I quit and you're a stupid-head."

"We don't say 'stupid,'" I said reflexively as Page flounced past me toward the backyard. "What was that about?" I asked Vanessa. She stared back at me with those big, green pools of eyes and said nothing.

"What's going on with those two?" I asked. Mom was in the kitchen, feeding baby Jack.

"Either too much time together or anxiety about being apart when Page moves out to Morrow Island for the summer," Mom answered. "I can't figure out which. Vanessa's mom is working the day shift, off tonight. Can you drive Vanessa home around seven? Sonny can't pick up Jack and Page until eight. I'd like to see those two separated and home in their own beds on the night before the last day of school."

"Sure. I have some things to do first, but I'll be back by seven." I started up the back steps, then stopped. "Why can't Emmy pick her up?"

"She doesn't have a car. A coworker who lives out on Thistle Island has been giving her rides to work, but she doesn't like to ask him to stop in town to pick up Vanessa."

I imagined life out on Thistle Island without a car. It couldn't be easy, especially in the winter.

In the clambake office, I started up the old desktop to check out the thing that had bugged me for two days. I had noticed the diamond ring, though neither Wyatt nor Chris had. It had arrested my attention because I was sure I had seen it before.

The reason we had the funds to even consider rebuilding Windsholme was because my mother had inherited a necklace. Called the Black Widow, it had an enormous black diamond as its center stone. Originally valued at two million dollars, the necklace had sold at auction to an anonymous bidder for five million. My mother had split the proceeds with two other heirs.

It wasn't the big black diamond I was interested in. It was the two dozen white diamonds rising up on either side of the necklace strand. I had photos of the Black Widow on my computer. They'd had to be sent off to the insurance company, the auction house, the attorneys, and a ton of other places. I found a photo and zoomed in on one of the white diamonds. The hair on my arms stood up. That was it! I was certain the diamond was the same.

I didn't recognize the stone, of course. I didn't have a jeweler's eye or experience. It was the distinctive, old-fashioned setting, an intricate filigree web. Someone had carefully transferred it to the ring, intact. I stared at the image for several minutes, even as I felt the tick of the clock. I needed to speak to Tom Flynn before Genevieve returned from the police station.

Le Roi jumped into my lap. He was too big for laps, but that was a premise he didn't accept. He settled, hind legs draped over one side, head and neck draped over the other, and began to purr. I petted him, sweeping the length of his chunky body. He was named Le Roi, for Elvis Presley, "the King," and in recent years, and especially this year after being an indoor cat for the whole of the winter, he'd come to resemble Vegas Elvis much more than Sun Records Elvis. But I could still feel the long muscles of his torso under the extra fat. "Sorry you've been neglected, old boy," I said, though he'd showed no resentment.

I searched the Web quickly to see if there was any news of the Black Widow. There wasn't. I knew the auction house wouldn't divulge who'd bought it. I'd tried that route before.

I had so many questions. Had Geoffrey Bower bought the necklace from my family at the auction? He must have. Did he know when he bought it he was coming to Busman's Harbor? He must have. The necklace had gone to auction in April. Wyatt had started work on the redesign of the *Garbo* the previous October. The refit would have been scheduled at Herndon's before then, possibly years earlier. I wondered so many things. Why had he bought the Black Widow? Did he know about its Busman's Harbor connection? And, if he did, why didn't he say anything to me about it when we met?

I moved Le Roi gently to the floor and searched for information about hemlock water dropwort. As Binder had said, it was highly poisonous. Symptoms would come on within an hour or so of ingesting it, terrible symptoms including vomiting and massive convulsions. As an interesting side note, scientists believed that it was the poison used to kill pesky, elderly relatives in ancient Sardinia, the origin of the expression "sardonic grin." Both Genevieve and Captain Marius had joined the *Garbo* in Sardinia. Coincidence? Probably.

But was there an antidote? There was, of sorts. Large doses of anticonvulsants given relatively soon after ingestion could save the victim. People had lived to tell the tale.

I looked for information about Geoffrey Bower.

As Quentin had said, for someone who'd made a huge financial killing, he'd managed to stay largely out of the press. There were notes about the *Garbo* on bulletin boards where people traded information about yacht sightings, and a few faraway shots through long lenses by paparazzi in Biarritz and Monaco who were no doubt hunting more glamorous prey. They showed the man I'd met, slightly pudgy wearing the yachtsman's clothing and cap.

Finally, I searched for information about the Alliance for a Fairer Universe. There was nothing. And nothing about Cliff Munroe either. Which struck me as a really funny way to run a protest group in the age of the Internet.

I knocked on the Snuggles' unlocked front screen door. Fee hurried out of the first-floor room in the back the sisters shared during the summer in order to maximize the number of bedrooms upstairs for rental.

"Julia!" She pushed her thick glasses back with her hand. Mackie stuck close on her heels as always.

"Is Flynn . . . er . . . Tom, here?"

"In his room, I think."

"Thanks." I dashed up the staircase before she could object. I realized at the top I didn't know his room number. "Tom!" I called on the landing. "Tom!"

There was a fumbling behind the door to room five. The knob turned and opened a crack. "Julia?" He was in jeans and a white undershirt.

I hurried over to his doorway. "You're trying to

find out what happened to Geoffrey Bower," I said. "On your own. Why?"

"I guess you'd better come in. Mind if I finish getting dressed?" He gestured toward a blue, plaid, cotton shirt laid out on the unmade bed. "Then shall we take a walk?"

I was embarrassed to have burst in on him like that. "Good idea."

He put on his shirt and stepped into a pair of brown loafers. As we left he called to Fee. "If Genevieve gets here before me, tell her I'll be right back."

He didn't say anything until we were near the top of the hill beyond Mom's house, starting down toward Gus's. "How did you know I'm asking questions about Bower's death?"

"Emil, the bodyguard, and Marius, the captain, both told me you'd talked to them. You're wearing jeans, clearly not working. You're freelancing. Captain Marius had the impression you were working with the state police. Can't you get in trouble?"

His mouth relaxed into a grin. "Only if I get caught."

Both Marius and Emil had told me with little prompting about Flynn's activities. They could easily tell others. "Why would you take that risk?"

He left the sidewalk and walked to the edge of the harbor where he stood on a boulder and stared down at the rocky, silty bottom. "Why are you talking to crew members?" He didn't look up at me.

"I told you. Quentin asked me to help Wyatt."

"You said you hadn't seen Wyatt in thirteen years.

You have a business to open in days. You'll have to do better than that to convince me."

I hesitated. "There is something else. I have a theory of how the crime happened. It all fits. I'll tell you, but only if you agree to work together. Two of us can cover more ground and learn more than each of us separately."

He surprised me by putting his hand on my shoulder, looking me in the eye. "You're trying to help Wyatt. My interest is Genevieve. What if one of us discovers something that incriminates one of them?"

"Genevieve's my friend too. Much more so than Wyatt. Besides, what does Genevieve have to worry about?" I asked. "I can't see she had a motive to kill Geoffrey, and she's dating the lead investigator's partner."

"She's been accused of murder before. By you, I believe."

"I was younger and more naive in those days."

Flynn rewarded me with one of his rare laughs. "You've grown since last fall." We went a few more steps and he continued. "Genevieve is scared to death she accidentally killed Bower. She's talking to Lieutenant Binder now."

"I don't think it was an accident, and neither does Lieutenant Binder. I've just come from talking with him. The state police are certain the crime was deliberate and I have a theory that fits."

"Did you run your idea by Lieutenant Binder?"

I shook my head. "I'm not ready to yet. I need more confirmation."

I unlocked the door to Gus's and walked Flynn to

one of the booths. Gus was gone for the day. The place was immaculate. My eyes swept the counter to see if there were any slices of Mrs. Gus's homemade pie left, but the glass shelves of the case were empty. I was disappointed but not surprised. I thought of offering soda or coffee, but I knew from experience Flynn would never touch the stuff. I sat opposite him, took a deep breath, and began. "You know I saw a diamond ring in the lobster's claw the night Geoffrey died."

He put his arms on the table and leaned forward. "I know you're the only one who saw it."

"There was a lot to see in that room. The food on the table, the awful grimace on the corpse. I noticed the diamond right away. I took that second look because I had seen that diamond before." I told him the story of the Black Widow. How my mother had received it and eventually sold it. About the anonymous bidder who'd bought it over the phone, and how I was convinced the diamond I'd seen the night of the murder was cut from the strand of the necklace. "I think Geoffrey had the Black Widow. In his safe. It was the motive for the murder."

"That seems crazy to me. Bower was worth billions. Why murder him to get a bauble worth five million?"

"Guys like Geoffrey, they don't go to their ATMs and pull out millions of dollars. When it comes to their money, they're essentially corporations. If he called his banker and told him to deliver five million in cash immediately to him on the *Garbo*, alarm bells would go off. Banks don't just do that. But the Black Widow is portable. Bower simply hands it over."

"It would be hard to fence."

"As a necklace, sure. But as individual gems? Only the center stone, the black diamond, is recognizable. It's your area, not mine, but I'm sure there's some Russian oligarch, some Chinese billionaire, someone who'd be willing to pay for it, no questions asked."

"Okay. I'll buy it. How do you think it went down? Why poison?"

"The killers put the poison in the curried chicken salad. The effects wouldn't kick in for an hour or more. His murderers confined Geoffrey in some way so he couldn't call for help and told him what he'd ingested. They promised him the antidote. All he had to do was give them the combination to his safe and let them take the necklace."

"But why didn't he tell them?" Flynn asked. "Why die for a five-million-dollar necklace if you're a billionaire?"

"Maybe he did tell them. Maybe they never intended to give him the antidote. Or maybe it didn't work or was too late. The only treatment is an anticonvulsant. That doesn't remove the poison from your system—it treats the symptoms. It's not an antidote exactly."

"How did the killers know he had the necklace?"

"For the same reason he trusted them to bring him

his lunch from the refrigerator. Because they worked for him," I said.

"You're supposed to be finding reasons it couldn't have been Genevieve or Wyatt."

"I know. But if the necklace was the motive, then our suspects are either people involved in the purchase of the necklace or its delivery to Bower, or the killers were someone who worked on that ship.

"Let's review the possibilities," I continued. "Captain Marius and Emil seem pretty tight. They claim they were together in Portland. Lieutenant Binder has confirmed they were in the Old Port in the early evening, but that leaves several hours unaccounted for. Ian, the mate, and Doug, the engineer, said they were around town all day. Again, the state police have several witnesses who saw them in bars, but can't account for the whole afternoon."

"Rick, the steward, seems like a lone wolf," Flynn said.

"Possibly. He claims he met up with Ian and Doug at Crowley's for dinner, but before that was at the beach on his own."

"Harder to check perhaps, but not impossible." Flynn was getting into it. Did that mean he believed me, or was at least entertaining the notion? "Then we have Maria Consuelo."

"Who's disappeared."

"There were two other possible killers aboard the *Garbo*," Flynn reminded me.

"Wyatt and Genevieve," I agreed. "Working together? Were they friends?"

"No, I don't think so. Not together. With another one of the crew. Or with an outsider."

That wasn't a road I wanted to go down. "The obvious outsiders are Wyatt working with Quentin—"

"And Genevieve with me," Flynn finished.

"Binder would never suspect you."

"He has to go where the clues take him."

"Which is not to you, not to Quentin, not to Genevieve."

"And not to Wyatt?"

I hesitated. "And not to Wyatt," I agreed.

"You're guessing about all of this." He didn't hide his skepticism.

I didn't blame him. I'd finally articulated my big theory and I could hear how outlandish it was. Except that it fit all the facts. Murder using a poison that took time to work. The necklace provided the motive.

"What about the ring?" Flynn asked. "Why leave it behind?"

"I don't know. I think it had something to do with the scene setting the psychologist talked about."

"Who made the ring?"

"That I think I do know," I answered. "Will you come with me to meet him?"

Flynn pulled his phone from his pocket and looked at it. "No text from Vieve. I'll come, if we can make this quick. We have dinner reservations at the Westclaw Inn tonight. I'm trying to get this romantic weekend back on track."

"The ring maker is nearby. If he tells us Geoffrey

had the Black Widow, will you help me convince
Lieutenant Binder to at least consider what I'm saying?"

"Of course," he said. "If I'm convinced."

We made it to the corner of Main and Main as Mr.
Gordon was locking up his shop. The jeweler peered
at me through his thick glasses. "Why, Julia, what
brings you here?"

"We have a matter of some urgency to talk to you
about. Can you stay for a little longer? This is—"

Mr. Gordon reached out a hand. "I know Sergeant
Flynn." They shook. Mr. Gordon glanced up and
down the street. "No reason to stay open late on a
Sunday evening this early in the season. The week-
enders have gone home. My wife has a pot roast on
the table for me, but I have a few minutes."

The three of us entered the shop. Both men looked
at me expectantly. "This is about the Black Widow,"
I started.

"Do tell." Mr. Gordon rubbed his stubbly chin.
When the necklace had first come to my mother, he
had authenticated it. Normally, the Black Widow
would have been a favorite topic, but I sensed his
wariness.

"Have you seen it recently?" I asked. "Did someone ask you to make a ring to match it using one of
its stones?"

"I don't think I should discuss that with you."
With his shaggy white hair, balding head, and round
cheeks, Mr. Gordon looked like a Christmas elf. But

he had a reputation as the soul of discretion. He sold engagement rings to nervous would-be grooms, and trinkets to cheating spouses. He knew who in town lived in genteel poverty, yet possessed priceless gems, and who lived like royalty, but brought their jewels to him for quick sale.

"I wouldn't ask"—I tried, and failed, to keep the pleading sound out of my voice—"but I believe the Black Widow is connected to the murder on the yacht in the harbor. And you know, Sergeant Flynn here is state police."

"Not in an official capacity," Flynn quickly clarified.

Mr. Gordon didn't seem to take note of the caveat. "I'll tell you," he conceded, "but only because you're connected to the Black Widow—and because he's here." He gestured in Flynn's direction. Flynn didn't see fit to clarify his role a second time. Mr. Gordon went on. "I have seen the necklace recently. A month or so ago, I was approached by an attorney who told me his client wanted to use one of the diamonds to make an engagement ring. Apparently he planned to offer the ring when he proposed and then provide the full necklace for the bride to wear on her wedding day.

"The attorney said they wanted me to create the ring because I'd dealt with the necklace before. That was a matter of public record. He believed I had the skill required. Also, his client was to arrive here in the harbor shortly."

"So you accepted the job," I prompted.

The jeweler nodded. "A courier delivered the necklace the day after I agreed. It was an easy enough job. The Black Widow has an abundance of possible stones. I took one from the top of the strand on each side, to keep the necklace symmetrical. I fashioned one of the diamonds I removed into the ring, keeping the filigree, so that the ring and the necklace would match."

"Do you have the necklace now?" I could barely speak. I was right!

"Heaven's, no. I put the ring in a ring box, and put the necklace, the extra diamond I'd removed, and the ring box into the purple case in which the Black Widow had been delivered."

"I know that case," I said, my heart beating faster. "That's how the auction company packaged the necklace. Did the same courier pick the jewels up?"

"No. It was someone else. The lawyer called ahead to say this man was coming. I showed this man the ring, and my work on the necklace ensuring the removal of the diamonds wouldn't show. He was most complimentary. Lovely man, with a French accent."

We thanked Mr. Gordon while he locked up the shop once again. He climbed into the ancient VW bug parked at the curb. As he drove off, I turned to Flynn. "French accent! He gave the Black Widow to Rick, the head steward. This proves my theory."

"It proves the part of your theory about the necklace, not the murder," he corrected.

"We have to talk to Rick."

Flynn looked at his phone. "Genevieve's back at

the Snuggles, wondering where I am. Our dinner reservation is for seven thirty. I'm not blowing this again."

"Seventy thirty!" I'd completely lost track. "What time is it now?"

"One minute after seven."

"I told my mom I'd drive Page's friend home at seven. Tomorrow morning we talk to Rick—I'm not kidding." I took off running.

Chapter 19

Vanessa was quiet on the drive to her trailer. I didn't know if she was tired or in a funk because she and Page had fought, so I let her be.

When I turned into their driveway, Emmy appeared on the top step of the trailer, the baby on her hip. She smiled and waved as Vanessa darted out of the car. "Thanks so much. Want a beer?"

"Yeah." I threw the emergency brake on the Caprice. "I'd love one."

Emmy disappeared into the trailer and came out with two bottles of Budweiser. The one I took from her hand was cold and sweaty with humidity. "Thanks."

"You look like you could use it." She sat down in the doorway of the trailer, the baby on her lap. I sat on the next step down. The baby was adorable, fat and smiling, a little older than my nephew Jack. He had his mother's coloring, blond curls and big blue eyes, not at all like Vanessa's long, tawny hair and the green eyes that haunted me.

Emmy moved her bottle to mine and *clinked* the necks. "Cheers," she said.

"Only one shift today?"

"Yes, thank goodness. Or not. I've struggled all spring with how little work they offered me. First they were only open weekends, then weeknights, finally now all day, every day. The tips are great, but the hours are brutal. That's why I so appreciate your mother's help in looking after Vanessa. Luther stays more or less still. My grandma doesn't have to chase him." To illustrate her point, she gestured across the yard to where Vanessa was running in circles around an empty, cracked birdbath. She hadn't been as tired as I thought. "By next year that will change. He'll be running around, but Vanessa should be old enough to help my grandma run after him. I just need to get through this summer. Somehow."

"Vanessa's really well behaved for my mom." The circus at the sleepover four nights before notwithstanding, she had been.

"Page is great for her," Emmy said. "Calms her down, balances her out."

Like all kids, my niece had her moments. "Page puts all her energy into the swim team."

Emmy took a pull on the beer. "Nessa needs something like that. Maybe dance or karate. Something to channel all that energy. Maybe next season, if I can make enough over the summer and find a winter gig. I'm glad she found Page. I worried about moving, especially in the middle of the year, but I had no choice."

"Where did you come from?"

"Phippsburg. My ex worked there. We had a little house."

"Vanessa mentioned the house." She hadn't mentioned the dad.

"She misses it. It's hard for her to understand. My husband lost his job, couldn't find another. He really tried. I give him that. I had to quit my job because of this guy." She jostled baby Luther on her knee, as if to say there were no hard feelings. "We fell behind on the mortgage. The bank foreclosed, we had to move, and Art, my husband, he—he fell apart." She smiled, but a brave smile, not a happy one. "My grandma had this trailer on her property. My dad lived here after my parents separated. Dad got a job down in Bath and he and his second wife moved out last fall." She looked around the property with satisfaction. "We got really, really lucky." It was hard to see it as luck, but she did. People did what they had to.

"Does Vanessa see her dad?" I asked.

"Art isn't Nessa's dad, but she lived with him for more than half her life. They love each other. He's in Portland now. He's got a part-time gig and an apartment. It's expensive down there. He has roommates, but he's hoping the job will turn into something, then he'll take Vanessa some when he takes Luther."

I'd finished my beer while she talked. Emmy took a last pull. "Want another?"

I pointed at the Caprice. "Better not. I'm driving and I have someplace else I need to go tonight before I head home. Thanks for the offer, though. I'm new in town myself. Came back last year after sixteen years away."

"A familiar story."

Not quite the same one, thank goodness. I'd been overwhelmed last year with the responsibility of a family business teetering on the brink of insolvency, but it was nothing like the personal upheaval Emmy had been through. "If you need a hand once my sister and her family move out to Morrow Island, give me a call. I can't guarantee I'll be around once the clam-bake season starts, but I'm in town a lot of nights waiting for Chris to finish work at Crowley's."

Emmy's eyes flickered with recognition, and something else I couldn't read. "He's a good guy."

"Yes," I said. "He is."

It was fully dark as I sped down lonely Westclaw Point Road toward Quentin's house. When I turned into his drive, my high beams illuminated the glare of the shiny granite building looming against the night sky like it had been thrust out of the rocks. The absence of lights shining from inside didn't mean Quentin wasn't home. Most of the windows and all of the living space were on the other side of the house, facing the water and Morrow Island. Quentin's station wagon was parked on the sandy track that served as his driveway.

I hoped the sound of my car would alert him to my arrival, so that he'd turn on the outdoor lights or even come out to greet me, but he didn't. When I switched off my headlights, blackness enveloped the car. I felt my way to the walk and up the steps to his deck.

By the time I made it halfway to the water side of the house, I saw the glow of indoor lighting from the giant windows that faced his deck and heard the sounds of a television. Quentin was home on a Sunday evening watching PBS, like millions of other people. I shook my shoulders to push away the tension, put a smile on my face, and knocked on the glass door. At the sound, Quentin's head snapped up, his features etched with surprise. But when he recognized me, his face relaxed into a grin.

"Julia," he said as he opened the door. "You gave me a start."

"People who live in glass houses—" I started.

"Shouldn't pick their noses while watching television," he chimed in, though he'd been doing nothing of the sort. "Come in."

He used the remote to turn off the TV. "Sit," he said. "Wine?"

"Not after my drive out on Westclaw Point Road. Water, maybe."

"Coming up." He slid behind us into the open kitchen. I heard the *whir* and *clunk* of the ice machine. "Not an impromptu social call, I take it?" He handed me a tall glass and sat opposite.

"Not entirely," I admitted. "Why didn't you tell me you were Wyatt's alibi for the afternoon Geoffrey was murdered?"

"Alibi?" His eyebrows shot up. "We're not to that point, surely."

"We may be past that point. Lieutenant Binder be-

lieves two people committed the murder. It would
have been difficult for a single person to have moved,
dressed, and staged Geoffrey's corpse. So Binder's
looking at the pairs of people who alibied one another that day. Emil and Marius, Doug and Ian,
Genevieve and Flynn, you and Wyatt. What did you
two do that afternoon?"

Quentin sat back, startled. "Are you honestly
asking if Wyatt and I killed Geoffrey Bower?"

I took a sip of the water, thinking about how to
form my vague worries into words. "No. I'm asking
if you're providing Wyatt with an alibi when she
has none."

He put his glass on the coffee table with more
force than necessary. "Absolutely not. I was with her
all day."

"Where were you?"

His gaze shifted from side to side, anywhere but
at me. "I picked her up at the boat at eleven thirty.
We were here all day. Or maybe we went to town. I
drove her over to Blount's a little before eight. It was
an unremarkable day, until Wyatt found Geoffrey."

"Is that how you answered Binder?" My voice
rose. "You *may* have gone to town? You're lucky you
haven't been charged with murder already."

"You're exaggerating."

I exhaled. Getting upset wouldn't help things. "I
am. For effect. I know you weren't here all day. I looked
over from Morrow Island at around two and your car
wasn't here. Where did you go?"

He let out an exasperated sigh. "All right. All

right. I took Wyatt to visit my parents. It's easily verifiable."

To visit his parents? I didn't believe him. "Is that what you told Binder?"

"Yes. Because it's true."

"You have parents nearby?" I was stunned. "You never talk about your family," I said. "You never say anything like, 'I'm off to visit my mom,' or 'Had a barbecue with my sister's family.' Do you even have a sister?"

"Julia, you're like a toddler who doesn't understand object permanence. Even when you can't see people, they still exist. They're off living their own lives."

"Very funny." I wasn't going to let him off the hook so easily. "But not an answer."

He raised a sandy eyebrow. "Long habits of a private person."

I wasn't placated. "It's called sharing your life. You do it with your friends. You certainly know everything there is to know about my family."

"You're right. I value our friendship. I'll do better. Yes, I have a sister, and a brother too. Both living here in town, married with kids. My mother was a lawyer. She's retired. My dad owned, still owns, the *Busman's Harbor Gazette*, though my brother-in-law runs it now."

I'd known his family was local in the sense that there were Tuppers all over the peninsula. I hadn't known he had close family right in town. I'd passed his mother's former law offices, which occupied the second story of Gordon's Jewelry, nearly every day.

The name TUPPER AND TUPPER was stenciled in gold on the window. Like everyone in Busman's Harbor, I read the *Gazette* every week. During tourist season I turned first to our print ad to make sure the placement was good, before going to the police report to find out what was up with my fellow citizens. I knew Tuppers owned it, but there were so many Tuppers in town, the branches spread out like octopus tentacles, I'd never taken the time to properly place Quentin, and he certainly hadn't seemed eager for me to do so.

"Why would you take Wyatt to visit your parents?" I asked.

"Because they became friendly when she and I dated, and she wanted to see them."

"When you *dated*?" I tried to disguise my surprise. I was sure Quentin was gay.

"I told you she worked on this house, and that's true. But really, I hired her firm because I knew her. She'd spent a year in New York between college and architecture school. She was the last woman I dated"—he paused as the seconds ticked by—"before I came out to my family."

"We've never had this conversation."

"I didn't think we needed to." He paused again, and then went on. "Wyatt was perfect. Ten years younger than me, naive, inexperienced. Undemanding. She was my unwitting beard. But when I broke up with her, she was stunned. And hurt. I made a real mess of it and I felt terrible. It was the final push to me coming out. Since then, I've tried to keep tabs on her, send business her way when I could." He

stopped, realizing what he'd said. "Not that that's
what I'm doing with your mother. Wyatt will be perfect for Windsholme."

I wasn't the least surprised Quentin was gay, but
the sophisticated Wyatt I knew—naive? Was it possible? What seemed sophisticated to me, as a ninth-
grader, probably wasn't real. But inexperienced,
even after college? Also possible. I had no idea what
path her life had taken after we parted company at
the age of eighteen. One thing Quentin's story did
prove: Wyatt had at least one previous relationship
with a wealthy, older man in which sex was nonexistent, or at least not an important feature. Perhaps
she had a type.

Quentin sat forward, putting his elbows on his
knees. "As long as we're here truth-telling, it's time
for you to tell me. Why are you so negative about
Wyatt?"

I thought about my reasons, and how I should ex-
plain them. "It's complicated, and happened long
ago, but the bottom line is, I don't trust her."

Quentin rose and collected our water glasses, carrying them to the kitchen. He returned with a bottle
of red wine and two elegant, stemmed glasses. "I
don't know if you're ready for this, but I need it." He
poured each of us a glass. "I understand complicated, believe me."

So I told him. About Wyatt and Lainey, Amber,
and Melissa and the luncheon we planned together
for Ms. Davis.

On the day of the luncheon, Wyatt had gone off to
get dressed in Lainey's room. She was borrowing a

dress from her and it seemed like a convenience. The plan was to meet in the common room of our dorm, where a limo we had hired would whisk us, along with Ms. Davis, to the inn.

I dressed with care, adding the single pearl drop necklace my parents had given me for middle school graduation to the plain blue dress. I counted my cash one last time, grabbed my coat, which was unfortunately a fluffy, maroon, down jacket, not the sophisticated wool coat a grown-up would wear, and anxiously headed downstairs. I was the first one to arrive.

Melissa arrived next. She was dressed in a simple but gorgeous wrap dress that hung on her perfectly. She eyed me with suspicion and didn't greet me. Was I inappropriately dressed? Self-conscious, but determined, I shrugged on the big down coat and zipped it closed. Amber came next and she and Melissa whispered together, glancing in my direction. Ms. Davis arrived through the front door. Melissa and Amber greeted her, and I went over to the little group to do the same.

Wyatt and Lainey came down last, laughing so noisily we could hear them in the stairway before we could see them. Wyatt stopped short at the bottom of the stairs, then came forward to say hi to Ms. Davis.

"Can I talk to you?" she whispered to me. "Over there?" She pointed to a far corner of the common room. I followed her over.

"What are you doing here?" she hissed.

For a moment, I truly was confused. "Going to

lunch." But before she said the words, I understood her meaning and my heart sank.

"You're not a part of this."

I fought to keep my face composed, but my eyes betrayed me. Tears sprang unbidden and rolled down my cheeks.

Wyatt's features softened. "I'm sorry, but we never invited you. The reservation is for five and that's all the town car can take. Otherwise—" She let her words hang in the air, as if she might have included me even then, but the logistics were too tricky. The rest of the group stared at us, the girls scowling, Ms. Davis with a look of confusion, like she didn't know what was going on, but knew it wasn't good.

Wyatt turned me around and gently shoved me toward the stairwell. "Our ride's here," she called brightly to the others.

"A week later a girl in another dorm dropped out of school," I told Quentin. "When I relayed my long, sad story to the housing officer, she felt so badly for me she decided I should have the girl's single room, even though I was a freshman and there were others more deserving. I moved out. End of story."

Quentin's face was solemn. He didn't laugh at the hijinks of teenaged Mean Girls or at my heartbreak. "I understand what it's like to be on the outside in high school. Did it ever get better for you?"

"I did make some friends, not many, but good ones." But mostly I studied hard, losing myself in my work. It became the habit of my lifetime, almost to the exclusion of everything else, until I'd moved back to Busman's Harbor the year before.

"And Wyatt?" Quentin asked. "Did she ever apologize?"

"There were only three hundred students in our school. Wyatt was unavoidable, though we never spoke a single word outside class or clubs. Except at graduation when she threw her arms around me and wished me all the best. 'My first roommate,' she called me. I've wondered since, was she saying she was sorry, or had she completely forgotten about that terrible day because it meant so little to her?"

To my enormous relief, Chris's truck was parked in Gus's lot when I got back to the apartment. I was exhausted and emotionally strung out from my conversation with Quentin. The only person in the world I wanted to see was Chris.

When I came up the stairs to the apartment, I was happy to find him awake, staring at a Red Sox game playing silently on our old television. He turned when he heard my footsteps. "Hey, beautiful." And then a frown. "What's the matter?"

So I told him. I told it all, about Quentin and Wyatt, and about Wyatt and me. He listened without interrupting, his arm around me, snuggled on the couch.

"So you see why I don't trust her?" I pressed.

"I see she hurt you." His deep voice was soft. I felt

the reassuring vibrations of his chest when he spoke. "But do you think she's capable of murder?"

"No, I don't. I do think I know how and why the murder was committed. After I got back from Morrow Island, I spent the rest of my afternoon on that. It has to do with the Black Widow." I explained about my theory, and my visit with Flynn to Mr. Gordon.

Chris whistled. "It's not a coincidence he bought the diamond and then came to town."

"No, I don't think so."

He was quiet for a moment, then he smiled. "Is that it? I'm not sure I can take much more."

I exhaled, moved out of his arms, and faced him. "Yes, one other thing."

He reached for my hand. "What is it?"

"I drove Vanessa home tonight." Did he look uneasy, or was I seeing something that wasn't there? "Have you noticed that child's eyes?"

"Yes," he admitted, looking down at the seat cushion. "They're exactly like my mother's."

"Your mother's?" It was strange that when he looked at Vanessa, he didn't see himself. Or maybe it wasn't. I wanted to shout, 'How would I know? I've never met your mother!' But instead I waited, barely breathing.

It took several moments, but then he pushed the words out in a rush. "I think Vanessa is my brother's daughter."

Brother? Is that what he said? "You don't have a brother."

He looked up from the couch cushion, straight into my eyes. "I do. He's ten years older."

"But you never mention him. You mention your parents, occasionally, when I push you, and your sister, once in a blue moon. You've never mentioned a brother. Does he live far away too? In Washington State, or Alaska?" The fourth corner of the country, as far away as possible from his parents in Florida, Chris in Maine and his sister in San Diego.

"He lives," Chris answered, "at the Maine State Prison at Warren."

We talked after that, or rather I fired questions at Chris while he paced around the studio apartment.

I was stunned. Stunned Chris had a brother. Stunned his brother was in prison. It took me a minute to get my bearings. Chris waited silently while I took it all in. "Why is he in prison?" I asked.

"Armed robbery."

"How much longer does he have to serve?"

"Five more years, last I heard."

"Was anyone hurt in the robbery?"

"No, thank God, not physically, but anything could have happened."

Chris had a brother. A brother he'd never mentioned. "How come you never told me?"

He stopped walking to look at me. "It's not something I'm proud of."

"It's not nothing either. And it's not like *you* were in prison. He's your brother."

Chris lost his patience. "My family's not like yours, Julia. My brother thought it was a good idea to take a sawed-off shotgun into a convenience store and demand all their money. It wasn't a good idea, it turns out."

An awful thought flickered. "Has everyone but me known this all along?"

He shrugged. "Sonny knows, I'm sure. He's never said anything?"

"Why didn't he tell me?" It really wasn't a question for Chris, whose sin of omission was the greater one.

"I'm guessing he thought it wasn't his to tell. Can we go to bed, please? I had a long day and I've got another one tomorrow."

I agreed, even though I knew I wouldn't sleep. While Chris fell quickly into a deep slumber, I stared into the darkness, wide awake, mind reeling. Twice in the same evening, men I loved had revealed they'd held things back from me about their families. Did that say something about me, or something about the men I let into my life?

I burned with questions. How, exactly, had Chris's family been unhappy? My family wasn't a barrel of laughs all the time either. My father had died too young. My mother had grieved long and hard. Livvie had gotten pregnant in high school. Sonny and I fought about the business. But none of it meant I would stay away from them. They were the best things in my life, along with Chris. The best thing, and the worst thing. Isn't that what families were to most people?

Chapter 20

Flynn's call woke me up the next morning. Once again the other side of the bed was empty and there was a text from Chris. OFF TO WORK. CALL ME LATER. I shook off sleep to answer my phone.

"You and I are meeting Rick Enrique for breakfast at Blount's," Flynn said as soon I answered. "Then Ian Cowen, followed by Doug Merriman."

"You've been busy."

He sped right on. "Lieutenant Binder's allowing the crew to go onto the *Garbo* to collect their personal belongings at eleven. I figure we'll roll right into that. Give Genevieve a hand with her things."

"And not incidentally get another look at the crime scene."

"Let's hope, though I'm sure we'll be closely supervised. See you in thirty minutes."

I was showered, dressed, and headed for the door when my cell buzzed.

"Hi, Mom."

"Julia, I'm glad I caught you." Mom sounded rushed and slightly breathless.

"Everything okay?"

"Yes, yes. I'm driving to the market. I just hung up the phone after talking to Wyatt. She's having a memorial gathering for Geoffrey Bower at four o'clock today at Foreman's. I'm going and I said I'd tell you about it."

That seemed impossibly soon. "Why on earth today?"

"She wants to do something before the crew leaves town. They're being allowed to take their personal things off the yacht today, and she expects some of them to leave as soon as they can."

That made sense. None of the crew had ties to the harbor. They'd have to move on, get other jobs. Binder couldn't hold any of them without an arrest.

"All right. I'm jogging past your house right now. I have to be at Blount's in seven minutes."

"Meet me at the house at three forty-five," Mom said. "We'll walk to Foreman's together."

Flynn was seated with Rick in a booth in Blount's coffee shop when I arrived. I waved the hostess off, indicating I'd located my party across the room. I fast-walked to their table, concerned that Flynn had started without me. The room was crowded with people eating breakfast, though I didn't see any other members of the *Garbo*'s crew.

It turned out Flynn and the steward were ordering. Their conversation hadn't gone beyond the introductions.

"You remember Julia Snowden," Flynn said to Rick as I sat down.

"Certainly. Her party was aboard the *Garbo* the night before Mr. Bower was killed. The first of many extraordinary events of the week." Rick said this in a neutral way, but I took his words to mean that somehow Chris, Quentin, and I had started a chain that led to Geoffrey Bower's death. I didn't see how that was possible.

"I understand you wish to talk," Rick said to Flynn in his soft French accent, "because the magnificent Chef Genevieve, your girlfriend, is upset her food was used to poison Mr. Bower." He pronounced Genevieve's name in the French way, making it sound even prettier and more musical than it was in English. He turned to me. "But, Ms. Snowden, what is your interest in the conversation?"

"Julia has helped the police with her inquiries in the past," Flynn interjected before I could speak. I worked to keep my eyebrows down. Always before, Flynn had characterized my contributions as "helping," the air quotes so pronounced you could practically see them hanging above his head. Not this time.

"And you are also a friend of Ms. Wyatt Jayne," Rick added, his mouth downturned.

"You're not a fan?" I asked.

Rick shrugged. His face was long and lean, his

goateed chin prominent. "I do not dislike Ms. Jayne. Life was good before she came. Then it was different. Change can be good, but not always."

"We understand you worked on the *Garbo* the second longest of the crew, over six years. Describe your relationship with Mr. Bower," Flynn said.

Rick rubbed his goatee. It was such an open-ended question, I wondered if it would produce any results. Finally, he spoke. "Mr. Bower is . . . was a very nice man. Wonderful boss. Easy to work for."

"Would you say you were confidants, friends?"

"I would say I was closer to him than most of the rest of the crew, except Emil, who has also been with him a long time. And because Mr. Bower and I have a special relationship, he sometimes asked me to do things of a personal nature."

"We understand he recently asked you to do one of those sorts of things. He asked you to go to Gordon's Jewelry and pick something up."

Rick's forehead creased in surprise. "How did you know?" Then his face settled. "You have spoken to the jeweler."

"Yes," I confirmed. "He told us he gave you a large purple case to take back to the ship, and he showed you the contents."

The waitress picked that moment to take our orders, a miracle of bad timing. Rick took his time responding to her, providing exacting requirements, how dark his toast should be, how hard the yolk of his egg. I sensed he was stalling. Finally, after filling our coffee cups and delivering the cream and sweeteners, she left us.

"Julia asked you about the purple case you picked up from Gordon's Jewelry," Flynn reminded him.

Rick took a long swallow of coffee. A plume of steam still rose from my cup and I wondered that he didn't burn his mouth. "The purple case," he said, setting down his cup. "Yes, I collected it from the jeweler."

"And then?" Flynn prompted.

"Why, I brought it immediately to the yacht. It will not do to be strolling through the town with something so valuable."

"And once you arrived at the *Garbo* what did you do with it?" I asked.

"I put it on the desk in Mr. Bower's office, which is a part of his stateroom, for him to later put it in the safe."

"How long did it sit there?" I asked.

"I don't know. Probably until much later that night. That is when Mr. Bower usually put things in the safe."

If the case sat there all day, any member of the crew might have seen it. "Mr. Gordon had showed you the necklace. You knew the contents of the case were extremely valuable. Why would you have left it out in the open?"

"This is what I always do when Mr. Bower is not in his office and I have possession of something that must go in the safe." Rick slapped his hand on the wooden table so hard I jumped in my chair. "Are you suggesting I am not good at my job? I have done everything I have been asked."

"Whoa, it's okay." Flynn tried to calm him. "We're trying to understand what happened. That's it."

But that wasn't good enough for me. "I'm sorry. I didn't mean to imply you weren't doing a good job. Mr. Gordon told us he showed you the necklace. You must have guessed how valuable it was. Perhaps it needed better handling than one of Mr. Bower's business documents?"

"Mr. Bower's business documents are sometimes more valuable than those gems," Rick pointed out. "Millions of dollars, hundreds of millions, ride on his transactions. We had no visitors on the boat. No one was going to steal from Mr. Bower. He would have known immediately it was one of us."

"When Mr. Gordon showed you the necklace, he also showed you the ring he had made to match it?" I asked.

The waitress came with our plates, more bad timing. Rick stabbed the yolk of his egg with his fork and sent it back to be recooked, repeating his specifications. "I will keep the toast," he added, so it must have met his standard for doneness.

I stared down at the oatmeal I'd ordered. It looked thoroughly unappetizing, though I couldn't decide if that was a function of the food or my mood. "The ring," I reminded Rick.

"Ah yes, the ring. Yes, I did see it."

"It looked like an engagement ring. What did you take from that?" I pressed.

"At first, nothing. Mr. Bower is a rich man. He can buy gems."

"But then?"

The waitress returned with his eggs. She waited while he cut into each of the yolks with his fork. The bright yellow insides ran out. "Perfection," he told her. *"Merci."* She breathed a sigh of relief, exiting quickly.

"The ring," I reminded him for a second time.

Flynn was nonchalantly cutting his egg white omelet into bite-sized pieces. If I hadn't known better, I would have thought he wasn't paying attention.

"All day as I am doing my chores, I got more and more curious about that ring. At night, when he put the purple case into the safe, I asked Mr. Bower about it."

I sat so far forward I almost dipped my chest in the oatmeal. "And?"

"He said he intended to give the ring to Ms. Jayne and ask her to marry him. It was then he told me about his plan for Friday evening. He wanted all the staff to leave the boat and Chef Genevieve to prepare a special meal."

"What did you think?"

Rick chewed a forkful of eggs slowly before he answered. "I told him I was unsure of the plan. He had not spent a lot of time with Ms. Jayne. I thought he might be rushing things. He told me the two of them had been corresponding and talking on the telephone for months. This was true. I had heard them once in a great while laughing and chatting as I cleaned his stateroom." Rick looked up toward the ceiling. "I am not sure I have ever heard him laugh, except on those phone calls. He was not a man of humor."

"Really?" The chatty, easy man I'd met seemed to have a normal sense of humor.

Rick backtracked. "Perhaps I exaggerate. Anyway, he was determined, so I wished him luck and said I would notify the staff of his wishes."

"Did Mr. Bower open the purple case before he put it in the safe?" Flynn asked.

"He did. He looked at the necklace and the ring, said the jeweler had done an artful job, opened the safe, and put the case in it."

The men finished their eggs. My oatmeal looked less and less appealing. Finally, Rick excused himself. "I have much to do before we go on the yacht to gather our things. It has been my home for six years and I have much there, even though my quarters are small."

Flynn and I stayed at the table after he left. "What did you think?" he asked.

"He's lying," I answered. "I'm not sure about what."

Flynn signaled the waitress to refill our coffees. "That's what I think too."

Ian Cowen appeared in the archway to the coffee room just after nine o'clock.

"I'll get him." Flynn stood, smoothing his cotton shirt over his jeans. At that moment, Doug Merriman arrived and greeted Ian.

"I thought you said we were meeting with them separately," I said.

"We were." Flynn didn't look happy. He returned to the table with the mate and the engineer.

"I hope you don't mind," Ian said with his broad Aussie accent. "Doug and I were chatting earlier and realized we were both scheduled to talk to you, so we came along together."

We did mind, especially since they were one of the pairs who alibied each other, but we also had no standing to compel either one to talk to us. We had to take what we got.

They were an odd pair. Ian was tanned, tall, and loose limbed, his blond hair always a mess. He slouched in his chair, to all appearances a laid-back Aussie. Doug was short, dark, and pale, well-proportioned, a miniature man. His movements were economical, his posture erect.

They ordered coffee and Flynn and I requested refills. I asked the waitress to take the congealing oatmeal away.

"I gather you want to talk about Bower's murder," Ian said "We've already spoken to the state police."

"Julia and I are helping our friends Genevieve and Wyatt gain a better understanding of what happened. That's all," Flynn reassured them.

"I can't think what we can tell you." Doug crossed his arms across his chest. Ian, on the other hand, leaned back in his chair, arms loose at his sides, apparently open to anything.

"I get that," Flynn said. "Bear with us. You left the *Garbo* together on Friday."

"Aye, aye," Ian said, grinning.

"At twelve oh five," Doug confirmed, demonstrating the engineer's love of precision, or a liar trying to get the smallest detail right.

Flynn pushed on. "And you were together from then until you were summoned to the *Garbo* Friday evening."

"We've been over this with the cops, minute by minute—where we were, what we did. We gave them receipts." Doug shifted forward in his chair. Was he going to leave? I could see the questions were aggravating. At the same time, Lieutenant Binder had said the police could account for only a portion of Ian and Doug's time away from the *Garbo*. Same with Emil and Marius. Same with Rick. Thanks to Quentin's revelations of the night before, I now knew where Wyatt had been for the whole period.

"How long have you been with Mr. Bower?" I asked Doug, easing us away from the discussion that had annoyed him.

"Three years."

"And before that?"

"Big yacht in the Mediterranean. Royalty on board. I'm not telling who. Before that, US Navy." He provided the answers at a "just the facts" clip.

The waitress brought their coffees and refilled Flynn's and my cup.

"How did you come to work on the *Garbo*?" Flynn followed up with Doug.

"A yacht staffing agency contacted me with the

opportunity and I jumped. She's a beauty." He hung his head. "She was going to be even more so when Herndon's got done with her, but now I guess that won't be."

"And you, Ian?" I prompted.

"Just joined in Portofino this year."

"Did you get your job the same way as Doug, through a yacht staffing agent?"

"Not exactly. Douglas and I worked together before, on our last boat. He rang me and said there was a crew job going begging. Recommended me for it."

So Doug and Ian had a prior connection.

"A lot of the crew left when they heard we'd be in some awful little town in Maine all summer—no offense," Doug added.

I was offended.

"The local cops are barking up the wrong tree talking to us crew all the time," Ian said. "If I was them, I'd be talking to that protester. The tall one."

"Cliff Munroe?" I asked. "Why him?"

"Is that his name? Why, aside from the fact that he hated Mr. Bower, there's him following the *Garbo* all over the world."

"All over the world?" Flynn confirmed.

"Yeah. I saw him in Capri when I picked up Ms. Jayne in the launch. And I swear I saw him standing on the quay in Sardinia behind Genevieve when I picked her up."

"Was he protesting against Geoffrey?" I asked.

"In Capri, yes, but in Sardinia, no. No signs or anything. He was just standing there," Ian said.

"You're sure?" Flynn asked, his voice eager. Ian nodded. "Did you tell this to Lieutenant Binder?"

"No, why would we have?" Ian was still slouched in the chair, but his voice was like steel. "He made it clear he was asking the questions."

Through the archway into the lobby, we could see the *Garbo*'s crew gathering. Doug looked anxiously at Ian.

"We've got to go," Ian said, standing up. "We don't want to miss our chance to get our stuff." Doug stood too.

"We're coming too." Flynn signaled to the waitress.

Doug and Ian walked out to Blount's lobby while I waited with Flynn as he paid the bill. "I talked to that protester," I said. "He told me his beef with Bower was personal."

"Why didn't you mention this before?"

"I was so focused on telling you my theory, I forgot about Cliff Munroe." He didn't fit a robbery motive. No wonder he was the professional detective and I wasn't.

Flynn threw two twenties on the table and stood. "We need to tell the lieutenant about this. And about the Black Widow. Hurry up."

Chapter 21

We joined the others in the lobby at Blount's and proceeded down to the dock as directed. All the crew members were there, along with Wyatt, Flynn, Quentin, and me. Quentin gave me an awkward smile, which I returned. Our discussion of the night before had taken some of the armor off each of us, exposing the tender skin beneath. We'd have to adjust to seeing each other in this new way.

Lieutenant Binder appeared ten minutes late, scowling as he hurried down the steps toward us. Jamie and Officer Howland were behind him, along with several state cops I didn't recognize.

"I apologize for keeping you waiting." Binder was composed, but cold. He didn't acknowledge anyone individually, not even Flynn. "Here's how this is going to work. You'll go straight to your quarters. An officer will accompany you. You will retrieve your personal items and your personal items only. The officer will inspect them and then escort you back to the dock."

"What if I don't agree to have my items inspected?" Doug asked.

"Then you can wait to get them until the *Garbo* has been through probate and has a rightful owner who can give you permission to go aboard." Binder was gruff, his patience thin to nonexistent. "Understood? Other questions."

Genevieve raised her hand. "I have personal belongings in the galley as well as in my cabin."

Binder looked at her for a moment, assessing. "Fine. Officer Dawes will escort you to the galley and to your quarters. Are your cooking items marked?"

"They have my initials on them," Genevieve answered.

"Very well."

Two of the state cops went up the gangway and slid back the hatch. We clustered at the bottom; the police moved to the top and stood on the open deck. "Go ahead," Binder said. One by one the crew started up. At the top, each crew member was paired with a state cop and then disappeared below deck, until Wyatt, Quentin, Genevieve, Flynn, and I remained on the dock, and only Jamie, Officer Howland, and Lieutenant Binder waited at the top of the gangway. Wyatt started up with Quentin behind her. "Why is Mr. Tupper here?" Binder asked. His voice was curious, not hostile.

"Quentin's here to help me carry my stuff," Wyatt answered. "In addition to clothes, I have a lot of work on board. Not just my work on the *Garbo*, other projects. I need to retrieve my files and drawings for my other clients. The drawings for the

Garbo are in Geoffrey's office. Legally, they belong to my firm. I'll have to be escorted there as well."

Binder frowned, but then gave a resigned nod. "Very well."

Genevieve climbed the gangway with Flynn and me following. "They're here to help me carry stuff too," she said, jerking her thumb back at us.

The lieutenant motioned to Jamie. "Officer, please accompany Ms. Pelletier and her entourage. Make sure they only go to the galley and Ms. Pelletier's cabin."

Great. He was on to us.

Genevieve led the way to the galley. We went down three sets of stairs, and through hallways that snaked around the ship's enormous engine and power plant. Thank goodness she was with us. Even though I'd been to the kitchen four days before, I couldn't imagine finding it on my own. Jamie, Flynn, and I stood in the crew dining area while Genevieve moved quickly around the small galley. She put a canvas holder with her knives on the countertop. A copper-bottomed pan used for poaching fish and a large pot followed. She lifted each of the pans to show Jamie her initials, GEP, marked on the bottoms. Into the big pot she put an empty olive oil dispenser, two wooden spoons, and a rubber spatula. She didn't show Jamie her name on those, nor did he ask.

"Did the crime scene techs clean out the refrigerator?" she asked as she opened the door. It was empty. The contents must have been taken for testing before they'd narrowed in on the salad. "What about the pantry?"

Before Jamie could answer, Genevieve disappeared inside it. He stepped up and stood behind her in the doorway.

"This all seems to be in order," she called.

"Ms. Pelletier, you have permission to retrieve your own things, period," Jamie reminded her. He waved us on impatiently. "Let's go. We still have to get your stuff from your cabin."

Flynn grabbed the big pot full of stuff and I took the poaching pan. Genevieve carried her own knives and led the way to her cabin, which was on the same level. In the cabin she pulled several uniforms out of the small built-in chest of drawers, polo shirts, long-sleeved shirts, sweatshirts, and a light jacket, all in the light aqua color and sporting the *Garbo* name. "Can I take these?" she asked Jamie. "They're provided by the ship's owner, but they're ours to keep. Besides I don't have enough clothes until I get back to my stuff in Portland."

"Sure," he said, but not before he glanced at Flynn, who nodded. "Sure." More confidently the second time.

Jamie inspected each item, including her underwear, before Genevieve put it all in a *Garbo* duffel bag, adding white pants and shorts from another drawer and her chef uniforms and toques. She gathered an e-reader from the top of the bureau and put it on top. "That's it," she said. "I took everything else with me when I got off on Friday."

"What's in the other two drawers?" I asked. I wondered if all crew members traveled as light.

"Maria Consuelo's things," Genevieve answered, her voice low. "What will happen to them?"

"If she turns up, I imagine they'll get back to her," Flynn said.

"I hope she's all right," Genevieve sighed. She took the big pot from Flynn and he shouldered the duffel bag.

"Are you sure you got everything?" I asked. "You didn't really check." For years we had moved from our house in the harbor to Morrow Island every spring and back again every fall. My mother had taught me to take one last look to make sure nothing was left behind. I opened the slim door to the closet. "Any of this yours?"

"Maria Consuelo's," Genevieve answered.

"What about this?" I pulled out a starched white apron.

"Ooh. You're right." She took it from me.

"See." I looked around again. It was a tiny cabin for two people. Not many places for stuff to hide.

"C'mon," Jamie urged. "The lieutenant will wonder what's happened to us."

"One more thing." I got down on my hands and knees, peering under the bed.

A pair of large brown eyes stared back at me.

"Aaaahhh!" I shrieked and she shrieked. The duffel hit the ground with a *whoomph* and Flynn was next to me, reaching under the bunk to pull Maria Consuelo out. She emerged, blinking in the dim light of the room, and then burst into noisy tears.

Genevieve, Flynn, and I waited on the hard benches across from the desk of the civilian receptionist at the police station. Finally, the door to the multi-purpose room opened and Lieutenant Binder stepped out. "She's shook up but otherwise fine. She says she stayed behind on the boat because she had nowhere else to go."

Genevieve made a strangled noise. "I never should have left her. I was so excited about having time off, seeing Tom. I didn't think about where she would go."

"She wasn't your responsibility," Flynn said sharply.

"She wasn't anyone's. That's why she got left behind," Genevieve snapped back.

Binder arched his back, stretching, as if he'd been sitting too long. His jacket was off, shirtsleeves rolled up, an unusually informal look for him. "She has the diamond ring." He looked at me when he said it. Then he looked toward Genevieve. "She hung out, napping in your quarters all afternoon on Friday. She got hungry and went toward the kitchen when she heard screaming coming from the dining room. That was Ms. Jayne discovering Mr. Bower's body. Ms. Lopez hid in the service pantry while Ms. Jayne called Mr. Tupper and then you. You and Mr. Durand arrived. You both escorted Ms. Jayne from the room. That's when Ms. Lopez crept into the dining room to see what had happened. She saw the ring in the lobster claw and stole it impulsively. She's been hiding on board ever since, going down into the bowels of the boat every time we searched, terrified we'd find out what she did. Today there were too many people on board. She got trapped in her cabin."

"She didn't see anyone else that day? Didn't hear the murder?" I asked.

Binder shook his head. "She swears no. Says she was asleep all afternoon. She's scared to death we're going to charge her with the theft of the ring. I believe she's telling all she knows."

"Can I see the ring?" I asked.

Binder looked up sharply. "Why? We've established you were right. The ring was there."

I looked at Flynn. Did he want to be included in this? His face was unreadable. I hesitated, hoping for a nod or a wink, or even for him to take over the conversation. He didn't, so I went on. "The reason I was so positive about the ring is because I recognized the diamond. Well, really, the antique setting it was in." I took a deep breath and went for it. "The diamond comes from a valuable necklace that belonged to my family." I glanced at Flynn again. "We've confirmed that Geoffrey had the necklace."

"We?"

Flynn finally spoke up. "I went with Julia to Gordon's Jewelry. Mr. Gordon fashioned the ring from a diamond on a necklace called the Black Widow. Then we spoke with Rick Enrique, the crew member who delivered the necklace to the *Garbo*."

"I believe the necklace may have been the motive for Geoffrey's murder," I finished.

"Unless the perpetrator was the protester, Cliff Munroe," Flynn added.

"It seems the three of us need to talk." He turned to Genevieve. "In the meantime, we've arranged for a room for Ms. Lopez at Blount's. Perhaps you would accompany her there and get her settled?"

"Of course." Genevieve stood.

"Meanwhile, Ms. Snowden, Sergeant Flynn, perhaps you'd like to share your insights on this case with me."

After we finished with Lieutenant Binder, I rushed back to Mom's to pick up the Caprice and drove out to Livvie's house. She and her family were moving out to the island the next day and I'd promised to help her with the packing.

We worked in Page's room, gathering the clothing and toys she'd need for the summer. Livvie listened, openmouthed, as I caught her up on my conversation with Binder and Flynn.

"Did Lieutenant Binder believe you?"

"I think so." I pulled a tangle of jeans out of Page's bottom drawer and sat on her bed to fold them. "Geoffrey's lawyer is arriving this afternoon. He has the combination to the safe and Lieutenant Binder says he'll open it. If the Black Widow isn't there—" I let the statement hang.

"The Black Widow," Livvie sighed. "Imagine." She was in the bottom of Page's closet pulling out summer shoes. "These won't fit." She held up a pair of sandals. "What about the protester?"

"Lieutenant Binder asked if I knew if he was still in the area and where he was staying. I only talked to him that one time. But they're looking for him."

"Mmm," Livvie responded, still from the bottom of the closet. "Any other news of the day?"

I stopped folding. "Chris has a brother in state prison."

That got her out of the closet. "What?"

"You didn't know? Chris said he was sure Sonny knew."

"It's never come up." I didn't believe her and said so. Livvie and Sonny were like conjoined twins who shared a central nervous system. "Seriously, it has never come up," she insisted. "I would have told you. What did he do?"

"Robbed a convenience store. With a gun."

Livvie dropped next to me on Page's bed. "Wow. Does Chris visit him?"

"I don't think so." But then I hadn't known about the brother either. "He doesn't like to talk about his family. But wait, there's more," I added. "The whole reason the subject of his brother came up was because I asked him about Vanessa."

"You didn't!"

"You told me to. You said that's what people in adult relationships did."

"Did I? I'm so sorry. You should never listen to me."

"Well, I did, and here's what I found out. He thinks Vanessa might be his brother's child."

Livvie's amber eyes opened wide. "Has he asked Emmy?"

"No, but I'm sure he's working up to it."

Down the hall, Jack began to babble in his bed. "Give him a minute," Livvie said. "He's happy." She patted my shoulder. "You've had an eventful twenty-four hours."

"Yup," I agreed. "And that's not even all of it. It turns out Wyatt used to be Quentin's girlfriend."

"WHAT?"

I filled her in on the whole conversation. At three o'clock, I rushed off to change and pick up Mom for the walk to Geoffrey Bower's memorial service at Foreman's Funeral Home. Livvie gave me a hug. "Thanks for your help. Tomorrow, Morrow Island!"

Chapter 22

Mom and I climbed the front steps to Foreman's, an old Victorian house on Main Street at the edge of downtown. The Foreman family had operated the funeral home and lived upstairs for generations. It was there that I had said my good-byes to my father and my grandparents. The Foremans had been seeing the Snowdens out of this world for a long time. The losses weighed on me whenever I crossed their threshold. I imagined it was the same for my mother.

A Foreman nephew greeted us and directed us to the larger of the home's two parlors. He wore a suit and tie, articles of clothing that had all but disappeared from Busman's Harbor in recent years. Lawyers wore them, but only on days they went to court. Politicians wore them, but only on days they went to Augusta. The men who sent you to your final rest were the only everyday suit-wearers remaining.

In the spacious front parlor, oriental carpets muffled footsteps and leather couches lined the walls. The center of the room had been set with rows upon rows of folding chairs, enough for a town dignitary. Who did Wyatt think would fill them?

Wyatt was at the front, waiting to greet people. Quentin stood next to her in a dark blazer. I was astonished to see the open coffin. Foreman's had the body for such a short time. Poor Geoffrey had been poisoned and then kept in the police morgue and autopsied. And there had been that awful grin.

My mother took my arm and dragged me to the front of the room. She hugged Wyatt, murmuring her condolences. I followed Mom's lead. "I couldn't let that horrible smile be the last I ever saw of Geoffrey," Wyatt whispered, answering my unasked question about the open coffin.

I turned and looked at him then. It was a standard wooden coffin, hardly befitting a billionaire. It must have been something Foreman's had in stock. The undertaker had done a good job with Geoffrey. I didn't want to linger on how they'd gotten rid of his grisly death mask, but he looked at peace. Only the top half of him showed in the split top coffin. He wore the yachtsman's blazer and cap, and the cheap wig, which was comically askew.

I felt badly for Wyatt, left to handle the funeral of someone she'd known long enough to care about, but surely not long enough to have discussed final arrangements. I wondered how specific Geoffrey's instructions had been. He seemed like a man who didn't leave things to chance.

Folks began filtering into the room. Rick, Ian, and Doug arrived together, Rick looking devastated, Ian and Doug stoic. They stopped short when they entered the room, no doubt as surprised by the open coffin as I'd been, but then made their way to the front. Wyatt greeted them. They gave their condolences, Rick kissing her on the cheek, then sat in the second row of folding chairs.

Genevieve, Flynn, and Maria Consuelo walked in moments later and joined their crewmates. All the crew wore their *Garbo* uniforms, a final tribute. Mom and I hugged Genevieve and shook hands with Flynn and the young stewardess, then moved to seats farther back in the room. Jamie and Officer Howland sat toward the back as well. Neither was in uniform and I wondered if they'd come out of respect or duty. I was a little surprised Binder wasn't present.

There was a scattering of other people in the seats, old townies who attended every funeral at Foreman's. I was oddly proud of the citizens of Busman's Harbor who'd had a chance to ogle the funeral of a murder victim and a billionaire, two potentially powerful draws, but who hadn't, more out of respect than disinterest, I hoped. Though it was Monday afternoon at the start of the busy season, so maybe practical considerations had kept the rubberneckers away.

Emil and Captain Marius were the last of the crew to arrive. They too reacted to the open coffin, especially Emil, whose mouth dropped. He caught himself, snapping it shut with a pop. They sat directly behind their crewmates.

I followed Wyatt's gaze to the back of the room. Cliff Munroe, the protester, sat on one of the couches that lined the back wall. Surely he wouldn't cause trouble at Geoffrey Bower's funeral. I turned back to Wyatt, who looked, not concerned, but puzzled. I remembered she'd never come out on deck during Thursday night's protest. Perhaps she didn't know who he was. Ian, the mate, had mentioned seeing Munroe in Capri, but if Wyatt had noticed him there, but had never seen him again, she probably wouldn't remember him in such a different setting.

Wyatt and Quentin took seats in the first row. The whispering mourners hushed. Mr. Foreman introduced Wyatt: "A friend of Mr. Bower who will say a few words of remembrance." She walked, shuffling a stack of blue index cards, to the lectern, where she faced us, drew a deep breath, and began to speak. "Thank you all for—"

The heavy pocket doors at the back of the room banged open. My head whipped around to look even as my brain told me it was impolite. Lieutenant Binder charged into the room, accompanied by a small man in a dark suit. Shaking off Binder's attempt to restrain him, he ran to the front of the room, shouting, "Stop! Stop!" Wyatt, and the rest of us, watched open-mouthed as he inspected the coffin. "This man is not Geoffrey Bower!"

The Foreman nephew reached Wyatt at the same moment Binder reached the dark-suited man. He turned back toward the assembled mourners, shrugging Binder off with an oath, while Wyatt fell into the funeral director's arms.

Everyone talked at once. "What is going on?" my mother hissed at me.

"I have no idea." I wished I was farther forward so

I could see the crew's reactions, but Flynn was there and he'd note them if Binder had his hands too full to do so. I turned around. Jamie and Howland had moved to the front to assist Binder. Cliff Munroe had disappeared.

At Mom's insistence we'd hustled Wyatt away while the police were occupied with the man in the suit. Wyatt sagged against Quentin's arm as they both sat on Mom's couch, her face a relief map of splotches and running makeup.

"Wyatt, I am so sorry," Quentin said. It was hard to know what to say. It was hard not to ask a million questions. Mom made a fuss about tea and cookies while I handed tissues across the coffee table.

"What did that man mean?" Wyatt finally asked with a last honk into a tissue.

"He said, 'This man is not Geoffrey Bower,'" I repeated, in case she hadn't heard in the melee.

"How could that be and who was that man?" she asked.

"He came in with Lieutenant Binder," I answered. "I think he might be Geoffrey's lawyer and business partner." It was pure speculation on my part, but we were in a situation short on established facts.

"Seebold Frederickson," Wyatt said. "Geoffrey talked about him all the time."

My mind swirled, chasing an explanation but unable to pin it down. If what the man at Foreman's said was true—if the corpse wasn't Bower—how many people were in on the conspiracy and how long had it been going on? The head steward, Rick, had been on the *Garbo* for six years, the security guard, Emil, for longer. Doug had worked on the yacht for three years. Everyone else was new.

Had Wyatt been the victim of the most elaborate catphishing hoax ever? One involving more than half a dozen people and millions of dollars to lure her to do—what? According to the crew, she hadn't even slept with the dead man. The more likely explanation was that the man in the church was the impostor. Lieutenant Binder was at that moment, no doubt, trying to untangle those questions of identity.

"Wyatt," I asked gently, "did you ever have reason to doubt Geoffrey was who he said he was?"

She was silent, wiping her eyes with a tissue she clutched in her hand. Quentin shot me a look that said, "Go easy on her." My mother reached over from the chair next to me and put her hand on my hand, the universal symbol for "hold back."

I understood their concerns. I tried again, as softly as I could. "Was there ever a moment when he said or did something that made you think, 'This doesn't seem right.'?"

"Geoffrey was eccentric, of course," Wyatt answered. "It took a while to figure out what was okay in his world and what wasn't. Sometimes there were contradictions. He never saw anyone in the flesh, but he would e-mail, text, and phone people all the time. Oh . . ." It seemed to occur to her what she'd just said.

"Did he video chat with other people, like he did with you?"

"I don't know. You should ask the crew."

I planned to.

There was a knock at the front door. When I opened it, Jamie stood on the top step. "Is Wyatt Jayne here? I've looked all over. The lieutenant needs to see her, pronto. And you too, Julia."

"I'm coming too," Quentin said.

Chapter 23

Quentin and I sat on the benches in the nearly empty police station while Lieutenant Binder met with Seebold Frederickson and Wyatt Jayne. While we waited, Flynn showed up.

"What's going on?" I asked him.

He didn't know any more than we did. "You got me." He sat down with us.

After almost an hour the door opened and Wyatt emerged, face stained with the salt of dried tears.

Lieutenant Binder followed. "Mr. Tupper, would you accompany Ms. Jayne to Blount's?"

"Of course." Quentin put an arm around Wyatt's shoulders and propelled her out the station door.

I stood, hoping to say something comforting to her, but her defeated look left me momentarily at a loss, and they were gone before I could get the words out.

"Julia, Tom, please come in," Binder said. "There is someone I want you to meet."

Inside the windowless multipurpose room the

man who'd made the scene at the funeral home rose from a folding chair. Lieutenant Binder closed the door behind us. "Mr. Frederickson, meet Julia Snowden and Sergeant Tom Flynn. They're the people I spoke to you about."

I stuck my hand out. "Thank you for seeing us."

"After what the lieutenant told me, about your theories about the case, I wanted to." It was my first real look at him aside from the fracas at the funeral home. He was a smallish man with light brown hair and large tortoiseshell glasses perched on an otherwise undistinguished nose.

Flynn put his hand out to be shaken too. "Police?" Frederickson asked.

"Maine State Police detective, Major Crimes," Flynn answered. "I'm on vacation this week."

Frederickson looked up at him, still holding his hand. "If you're on vacation, what's your interest in Geoffrey?"

"My girlfriend is Genevieve Pelletier."

Frederickson released his hand and nodded. "Ah, the chef. I've heard only good things about her. Okay if we sit?" he asked Binder. The four of us arranged the metal chairs into a rough approximation of a circle. "What's your interest in all this?" he asked me.

"I went to school with Wyatt Jayne," I answered. "I was the person she called when she found Geoffrey. I have another interest, as well, but let's talk about it in a bit." I cleared my throat. "Maybe it would help us all understand and get on the same page if you told us something about your relationship with him."

The lawyer looked at Lieutenant Binder, who nodded.

"In addition to being Geoffrey's friend, I'm his attorney," Frederickson said. "I've already disclosed to the lieutenant everything I'm obligated to. I won't tell you anything I deem confidential."

"Fair enough," Flynn responded.

Seebold Frederickson leaned back in his chair, like a man getting comfortable to tell a long story. "I met Geoffrey when my parents moved me into his elementary school district when I was nine. He was a strange kid even then. A genius with numbers, fascinated by patterns, but socially awkward. Before we met, I don't think he'd ever had a single friend, but I don't think he cared either. The other kids were vaguely repulsed, but I was attracted like a magnet. I'd never seen a mind like his. His enthusiasms were fascinating. We went through a space phase when we built real rockets, a collectible game cards phase, when his parents drove us to tournaments all over the state. I understood that there was no room in the relationship for my separate hobbies or interests, but as long as I was willing to go along for the ride, he'd let me.

"He discovered the stock and commodity markets when we were sixteen. He was accepted at MIT, but declined so he could focus on investing. I took a more traditional route, college and then law school. Afterward, he asked me to set up his firm, so he could invest for a limited number of others. It took boning up and a lot of complex corporate and securities law, but I was successful. I've worked for

Geoffrey exclusively ever since." He went to the bubbler on the other side of the room, extracted a funnel-shaped paper cup from the holder, and filled it with water. "Is that the sort of thing you want to know?"

"Partially," I answered. "I'm still trying to work it out. At some point the man in the coffin became Geoffrey. Did you know?"

Frederickson put down his cup, nodding as he did. "Absolutely. I facilitated it."

"Then why were you surprised by the identity of the victim today?"

"We'll come to that." He drained the cup in a single swallow. "After he made a killing in the housing collapse, Geoffrey got what he considered an undue amount of attention. He managed to stay out of the major books and movies and avoided having his photo in the paper, but even the articles that appeared in the financial press were too much for him. Whether you think what he did was horrible or an act of financial genius, it was all too public for such a private man. He purchased the *Garbo* and moved aboard, roaming the earth. His investment business is incorporated in the US, but he is essentially stateless. He still invests for himself and his clients, but I have become the public face of the company. He was a shy man who became a true recluse. His parents were gone. His only real tie was to me. Leaving his identity behind was the next step, a momentous, but not an inconsistent one."

"All because of a little publicity?" I asked. Geoffrey's behavior was extreme.

"It was more than that. Even though Geoffrey wasn't as well known, there was a constant stream of nasty e-mails, letters, public postings. I've read many." The lawyer shuddered. "They are horrific. Some of them threaten physical torture, graphically described. And then there are the sad ones. They're worse than the threats. Long tales of houses, jobs, and health lost. Hope lost. Some beg for money, but most solely want him to know that his gain has been their catastrophic loss. Geoffrey felt guilty about the money. He was plagued with guilt."

"So you hired whoever was in the coffin," I said.

"I did."

"Unless he had a very hard life, that man was older than Geoffrey," Flynn observed.

"A little of both. Geoffrey asked me to go through the e-mails and letters and find someone deserving, capable, and appropriate to take over his life. It was like looking for a needle in a haystack. Eventually, I found Bert Sand, a former character actor, never successful enough to be recognized, who thought he'd found his way out of the acting game and into making a fortune by flipping houses in Orange County, California, during the boom. Bert made a lot of money at first, but like most people, he thought the good times would roll forever, the price of property would never go down. He invested in higher and higher end projects, until it all came crashing down. He lost his money, his home, his wife.

"When I first tracked him down, I thought I'd find a shadow of a man, but Sand was a congenital optimist, friendly, charming, and more than eager to take on a life with no expenses, where he could bank his pay and visit some of the most glamorous places in the world."

"Even though he couldn't go ashore?" I asked.

"He did go ashore sometimes, when Geoffrey didn't need him to be seen on the boat. It was easy for Bert to do it. Once they got him off the boat, all he had to do was go back to being himself—a short, bald man in his fifties, no connection to Geoffrey Bower."

"Bert didn't look like Bower?" Flynn seemed surprised.

Frederickson laughed a hollow little laugh. "Not hardly. Geoffrey's my age, more than a decade younger than Bert. And he's tall and good-looking. I always thought his handsomeness was so annoyingly wasted on someone with no interest in attracting other humans." He paused, gathering his thoughts. "I think Geoffrey saw Bert's homeliness as a plus. Geoffrey made a fortune in his late teens and a humongous fortune in his thirties. His relationships were never easy, and after he was rich, he never trusted people to like him for himself. He suspected they wanted something from him and he was usually right. I'm sure that was part of what turned him away from the world. There were a few women who threw themselves at him, before he moved permanently to the *Garbo*. He never showed the slightest interest. I think for Geoffrey, Wyatt loving him, in spite of thinking he looked like Bert, was like a test she passed."

A reverse Cyrano. "How long has this charade been going on?" I asked.

"A little over four years."

I thought back through our conversations. "So Rick, the steward, knew, and Emil, the security guy, knew."

"Yes, Rick and Emil were the only members of the crew who knew the secret. Everyone else has been hired since Bert stepped in. We've had, in fact, two captains since Bert took over the role."

"Where has the real Geoffrey been all this time?"

Frederickson shook his head. "I never really know. Until last Friday, he was always available to me via voice mail, e-mail, and text." He raised and lowered his shoulders. "I accepted his location as something I was not to know. I do know he sometimes followed the ship, staying in the same ports, because he was needed to sign documents related to his business that were couriered to the boat. I would ask him where to send the stuff, and he would say, always, 'Send it to the *Garbo*, care of this or that harbormaster.'"

"What happens to Bert Sand now?" Flynn asked.

Frederickson pointed to a laptop sitting on another chair. "I've gone through my paperwork from when we originally hired him. I was able to locate a niece and nephew, children of an estranged sister. Lieutenant Binder was kind enough to call the young woman."

"How did she react?" I asked.

"She was thrilled someone else paid the burial

expenses for an uncle she and her brother didn't know they had," Binder answered. "I'm sure they'll happily split the salary Bert banked once everything is sorted out."

"When you arrived today, who did you think was dead?" Flynn asked the lawyer. "Why didn't you put a stop to the funeral earlier?"

"It never occurred to me Ms. Jayne would hold the funeral so soon. I thought I had time to deal with these matters. I hadn't been able to reach either Bert or Geoffrey. Neither Rick nor Emil had seen the body. Ms. Jayne had discovered the body, and from all that happened after, we assumed it was Bert. But there was a chance it wasn't. Geoffrey had planned to reveal himself to her on Friday, the day the body was found. I didn't think he had, but I couldn't be sure. I didn't know if my client was living or dead, or what my obligations were for confidentiality."

"Why didn't Rick Enrique or Emil Nicolescu say something?" Flynn was clearly annoyed, as he would have been in his official role.

"I asked Rick and Emil to wait until I arrived to tell the police the whole story. Like me, they couldn't reach either Geoffrey or Bert, and like me, they didn't see the body until they got to the funeral home today. But there's another reason. They have both signed confidentiality agreements that give them huge bonuses for every year they keep the secret."

"Why did Bower plan to tell Ms. Jayne the truth? Why then?" Flynn asked.

I bounced in my seat. "Because he was about to propose to her."

Frederickson looked down at his hands. "I believe so."

"Geoffrey wrote the e-mail and the cards," I guessed. "He was on the other end of the text conversations and the all-night phone calls. He sent the flowers and the gifts. He collaborated on the plans for the *Garbo*. He fell in love with Wyatt. But what about the video conferences?" I asked.

"Bert Sand did those," Frederickson answered, "but within tight guidelines. Sometimes he'd mute the call like he was conferring with Rick, though actually he was getting the answer to a question Ms. Jayne had asked about the refit. Bert was a gifted mimic. Their voices were similar enough, at long distances, over the Internet . . ." Frederickson's voice trailed off.

"When Bert Sand was killed, why didn't Bower himself come forward? It's more than some silly game at that point," Flynn pressed.

"I don't know." Frederickson stared at his hands. "I don't know why he didn't return my calls, or Emil's or Rick's. If I had to guess, I'd say Geoffrey contemplated staying dead. At some level, it was the ultimate solution for his desire to disappear. But he's thought better of it. He's finally answered my texts. He's coming to talk to Lieutenant Binder and tell him what he knows. He's arriving within the hour."

"Arriving how?" Flynn asked

"I don't know. He can't be far from here if he was going to reveal himself to Wyatt last Friday night."

"How did you know Geoffrey was going to ask Wyatt to marry him?" I asked.

The lawyer hesitated. I thought he might claim attorney-client privilege. His client was alive. But after a minute or so, he went on. "Two reasons. Geoffrey had created a foundation to provide housing to people in need. Last month he changed his will and left Wyatt in charge of it in the event of his death. That seemed like a big deal to me, more like something you'd ask of a family member. When I questioned him about it, he told me not to worry—I'd understand everything soon."

"How could he have thought she would agree to marry him? His deception was so enormous. I'd have—" I floundered, at a loss for words.

"Killed him?" Binder prompted, then smiled as I stammered.

Frederickson went to the water bubbler again and filled his cup. He returned to his chair and looked at Binder, who nodded for him to go on. "I've described Geoffrey's life to you. Even before he 'disappeared' it was one of extreme isolation. I am, as I said, his only friend. He's never dated, never been in love. Never showed the slightest inclination, truth be told. I always assumed he was uninterested. Given his lack of experience, it's not surprising he thought Ms. Jayne would be delighted and persuaded by his big reveal. To me, it's more surprising he wanted to do it in the first place."

"You said there were two reasons you knew Geoffrey planned to marry," Flynn reminded him.

"He also asked me to acquire a piece of antique woman's jewelry."

"A necklace," I said. "The Black Widow."

Frederickson nodded. "How did you know?"

"Long story. I recognized the setting of the diamond ring when I saw it on the table at the . . ."

"Scene of the crime," Flynn finished for me.

The lawyer didn't respond. Clearly he wasn't satisfied with my answer, so I continued, filling in the blanks with my guesses. "You acquired the necklace at auction, last April. Right after Wyatt visited Geoffrey . . . er . . . Bert Sand on the boat the second time."

Frederickson relaxed, smiling. "So you're not clairvoyant. I bought it for Geoffrey a little over a month ago, as the *Garbo* was crossing the Atlantic. From a private owner. We paid way too much for it, but the owner had overpaid for it not long before."

Now it was my turn to be surprised. Geoffrey hadn't bought the Black Widow at the auction. He'd bought it from whoever had bought it at auction, or perhaps there were several steps in between.

"He had me send the Black Widow via private courier to a jeweler here in town who was familiar with the necklace," the lawyer continued. "The jeweler fashioned the engagement ring from one of the stones near the top of the strand."

"Why buy a necklace if he wanted a ring?" I asked.

"As I understand it, the necklace had ties to Busman's Harbor. That's the kind of thing that would appeal to Geoffrey. And, I think the ring was meant to symbolize the promise, and eventually the necklace was to symbolize the more to come." He stopped speaking and looked at me, the light slowing dawning. "So that's why you know about the necklace. It belonged to your family."

I admitted it. "Yes, my mother was a part-owner of the Black Widow. It's an unfortunate name for a piece of jewelry. Especially for poor Wyatt. Do you know where the necklace is now?"

"As I said, Lieutenant Binder has told me about your robbery theory. When Geoffrey gets here, the lieutenant is going to accompany us to the *Garbo* to check on the safe."

"Did Bert Sand know the combination to the safe?" Flynn asked.

"No. Only Geoffrey and me. He traveled extensively and couldn't carry much with him. When he'd go onto the ship to sign documents in the middle of the night, he'd leave his copies in the safe."

"I suppose you wouldn't tell me whom you purchased the Black Widow from," I said.

Frederickson shrugged. "Don't see why not. Nothing about the transaction was confidential."

I sat forward in my chair. I'd wondered about the anonymous bidder on the phone since the day of the auction.

"It was a local guy," Frederickson said.

My heart beat faster. I thought I knew what was coming.

"Name of Quentin Tupper."

Indeed. I stood. "I'd have to go, I need—"

Binder's phone rang. The lieutenant went to his

makeshift desk, picked up the receiver, and listened to the person on the other end. "Send him in," he said.

The door opened and Cliff Munroe entered, the tall, handsome protester.

"Lieutenant Binder?" He looked from Flynn to Binder and back again. "I'm Geoffrey Bower."

Chapter 24

Lieutenant Binder invited Flynn and me to leave the room immediately after the real Geoffrey showed up. My mind swirled, full of unanswered questions about Geoffrey Bower, Seebold Frederickson, Bert Sand, and Cliff Munroe. But one thing, a more personal thing, had the most urgency.

We stood in the twilight on the sidewalk in front of the police station while I dialed Quentin's cell. "Where are you?" I listened and finally said, "Stay. I'll be right there."

"Quentin's in Wyatt's room at Blount's," I told Flynn. "Genevieve and Maria Consuelo are there too. It's turned into an impromptu wake for the man they knew as Geoffrey Bower."

"I'm coming with you," he said.

I put my foot down. "This part of the story doesn't concern you. This is between me and Quentin."

"I mean I'm coming to Blount's. I want to check in with Genevieve and then I'll wait on the dock by the *Garbo*. If I'm there when the lieutenant arrives with Frederickson and Bower, I'm pretty sure I can talk him into letting me watch them open the safe."

"Us," I corrected. "Letting *us* watch."

"That'll be a harder case to make," he warned. Then scanning my expression, he added, "Meet me on the dock when you're done with Quentin."

When Wyatt opened her hotel room door, I beckoned across the room to Quentin. "Let's go downstairs. We need to talk." As we left, Flynn slipped into the room.

We found a quiet corner in the bar. "Most mysterious," he joked. "What is this about?"

I pounced. "You bought the Black Widow. You were the anonymous bidder on the phone at the auction. You sold the necklace to Geoffrey Bower."

Whatever he'd been expecting, that wasn't it. Even in the low light of the bar, I could see the color drain from behind his tan. "How did you find out? Why would Bower buy it?"

"Because it was local and historical and that's the kind of thing he likes, according to his lawyer. Don't change the subject. We're talking about why *you* bought it." I waited.

"I did buy the Black Widow at auction," he admitted.

Even though I'd guessed, the news hit me like a plank to the chest. "But why?"

"Because I wanted your family to rebuild Windsholme and I thought the surest way to make it happen was to get enough money into your mother's hands. When she inherited the Black Widow, I saw my chance."

A waitress hovered nearby, waiting for our drink order. Quentin waved her off.

"Why do you care if we rebuild it?" I asked. "You can only see the upper stories from your house."

Again, Quentin didn't speak for a long time. When he did, his voice was thick with emotion. "If you didn't rebuild it, you would knock it down. It would disappear."

It still didn't make sense. Demolishing the mansion wouldn't ruin Quentin's view. Someone who'd never seen the view before would never know Windsholme was missing. "Why is that so important to you?" I waited impatiently as the minutes ticked by.

"Did you ever wonder why I built my house on that spot, looking out at your island?" he asked.

"You've said the land was in your family." Quentin's modern fortress had replaced a shack built to secure his family's claim to lobster in the narrows between Westclaw Point and Morrow Island.

"That's true, but there's a more personal reason. It has to do with our discussion last night."

"That you're gay."

"Yes, but I was thinking more about the topic of personal disclosure. My explanation involves a personal disclosure."

I settled into the booth. "I'm waiting."

He'd left his blazer in Wyatt's room. He was in his usual blue cotton shirt, sleeves rolled up. He put his elbows on the table and began. "Like a lot of gay

teenagers not yet out, I believed I was going to be a
grave disappointment to my parents in one way, so I
overachieved at everything else. I didn't think it was
ever possible that I would marry or give them grand-
children, so I became the best at academics, sports,
volunteering, Scouts. The most helpful around the
house. The kid the other parents relied on. The one
they said, 'Okay, if Quentin is going, you can too.
But stay close to him and stay out of trouble.' It was
wonderful, because I was admired and praised. And
it was exhausting because I was simultaneously keeping a giant secret and striving so hard."

I nodded to show I understood. It would be a
struggle to be the perfect teenager and to keep such
a huge secret at the same time. Either one would be
exhausting on its own.

"My uncle was the black sheep of the family. Never
went to college. Never married. A good lobsterman
with a quiet life. He stayed all summer in that shack
on the land where I built my house. By the time I
remember, it had electricity and running water, but
barely. I don't know how the tradition started, but
every summer, he'd have me out there for two weeks.
Just me. Not my sister, not my brother. We worked
hard every day I was there. We'd get up at four in the
morning to pull his traps, be out on the water for hours.
Then go to the lobster co-op to sell the catch and
finally home to endless chores of scrubbing down the
boat, fixing traps, painting buoys.

"I was never happier than I was those two weeks
every summer. It was fourteen days of the year when

I followed my uncle's lead, did what he told me, and didn't have to pretend I was something I was not."

"But Windsholme—" I interrupted. This was all very interesting, the kind of confidence I would have loved receiving from Quentin in any other circumstance, but I didn't want to stray too far from the Black Widow.

"I'm getting to that. Have some patience, Julia." He waited to make sure I wasn't going to interrupt again, then continued. "I'd fall into bed exhausted every night. It was summer, so the days were long. We got up so early that even as a teenager I went to bed in twilight. The window by my bed looked out on Morrow Island. I'd fall asleep every night staring at Windsholme, thinking about how happy I was and how I wished the summer would never end."

I thought about that teenaged Quentin, staring at Windsholme. I'd stood on the boulder on the little beach on Morrow Island so many times, staring in the other direction, at the lobster shack on the rocky piece of land across the narrows. Quentin was a dozen years older than me. When Livvie and I were old enough to go off on our own, but too young to work at the clambake, we'd often clamber over that boulder at dusk while our parents and their employees fed the day's second boatload of tourists their lobster dinners. Had Quentin been in that shack, staring in my direction at the same time? We hadn't met until a year ago, even though we'd lived in the same town for years, and then two blocks apart in Manhattan for years more.

"And your uncle?" I asked.

"Stayed up drinking. I slept so soundly, I never heard him go to bed. He died when I was in college and left me the land and the shack. Cirrhosis. My life was changing radically by then."

"You were rich." Quentin, a classics major, had built a tiny piece of computer code in college that made all the software in all the world run more efficiently. Or so it seemed. He'd lived off the royalties ever since.

He nodded. "Not yet, but I was on my way to being. I didn't come out to my family, or anyone else, for another decade. But when I did, it was a huge relief. The charade was over."

"And your family was—?"

"Not surprised." He laughed again, an easier laugh. "Evidently, I wasn't keeping the secret quite as adeptly as I thought. Anyway, I didn't do anything with the land for a long time. During my thirties, I traveled. I thought I had everything, but I didn't have anything that was meaningful. Few friends. No work. No relationship. No family. Building the house on Westclaw Point, coming back to the place I was happiest, was supposed to be a start at finding all I'd missed."

I reached across the table and squeezed his hand. My dear friend. "You've explained you have a sentimental attachment to your view. But what about the Black Widow? That was a crazy amount of money to spend on a gamble my mother would use it to fix the mansion."

"You know money doesn't mean much to me."

"That's what people say when they have plenty of it."

"Touché."

"But then you sold it," I said.

"I didn't need the necklace. I knew your family wouldn't take it back. I was approached by Seebold Frederickson. I never met him. We talked on the phone. Funds were exchanged electronically. He never said whom he represented. I sold the Black Widow to the something-or-other trust. I did try to hedge my big bet by introducing your mom to Wyatt. I knew she could convince your mother Windsholme should be rebuilt."

"And now look where that's got us," I said.

"Indeed," Quentin responded. "Though I'm starting to enjoy our nightly talks."

Chapter 25

I found Flynn sitting on the dock across from the *Garbo*. The overhead lights left pools of illumination on the rough boards, but he sat in a darkened corner, his back to Blount's retaining wall.

"Sit down," he said softly, careful so his voice didn't carry on the water. "This could be a while. The lieutenant will have a long interview with Bower and Frederickson before they come over here."

"Are you sure they'll come?"

"Lieutenant Binder will want that safe opened tonight." He paused. "You realize that since the killers poisoned the wrong man, we should now expect to find the necklace still in the safe. Bert couldn't have given his murderers the combination."

"I worked that out. Poor Bert."

"After you left with Tupper, I told Wyatt we'd met the real Bower," he said to me.

"Won't the lieutenant be mad you did that? He probably wanted to see her reaction."

He sighed. "Yes, probably, but I couldn't sit in that

room with her, knowing what I knew, and not tell her. She's been deceived enough."

"It's a little different on the outside looking in, isn't it? How did she react?"

"About as you'd expect. The poor woman is a mess."

We lapsed into silence. Sitting in close proximity, in the dark, got more uncomfortable as the moments ticked by. "Why did you leave Providence?" I kept my voice low, as he had done. I knew his father was a chief on the force there. His brother was high up too. They were a whole family of Rhode Island cops. Why leave?

"I did join the Providence police when I was in the army reserves. I went to Afghanistan and came back. I felt like I didn't fit in. In the police force or in the family. I needed to get away. The Maine State Police were hiring. Here I am."

"Didn't fit in? You'll have to do better than that."

He didn't answer for so long, I thought he might not. But then he said, "My brother married my girl-friend while I was deployed."

I was surprised. Flynn of all people. The man of few words who had everything under control. "I'm sorry."

"Don't be. It gave me the kick in the rear I needed to leave town. I have so many relatives on the Providence PD, I was bound to be reporting to one or another my entire career. Besides, all's well that ends well. Or at least I hope it is. I've asked Genevieve to marry me."

I inhaled sharply. In the dark I could feel him shift his body to face me.

"She didn't tell you?" he asked.

"No. When was this?"

"I planned to do it at dinner Friday night, but she got the call with the news about the murder. I think she suspected my proposal was coming, even before Friday."

I remembered how Genevieve had thrown her arms around me Thursday night on the *Garbo*, like I was a long lost friend. Or a life raft in a raging river.

"I finally completed the proposal last night," Flynn continued. "I was sure you figured out what was going on when Mr. Gordon said he already knew me."

I hadn't even suspected. "I was preoccupied at the time. What did Genevieve say?"

"She asked for time. I get it. She's younger than me. She's worked every day of her life since she was in high school. I'm ready to settle down, have a real life. I hope she is. I love her, Julia. I really do."

In the darkness, I flushed at the intimacy of his declaration. This was a new side to Flynn. "She's fantastic. For what it's worth, I think you'd be a great couple. Good luck." I was touched that he'd confided in me about something that made him so vulnerable. We lapsed into silence again.

"What about you?" His hushed voice startled me in the darkness, even though I knew he was there.

"What?"

"What about you and Chris? What's going on there? I can never get a handle on you guys. Is it serious? Do you think you'll marry him?"

"I know you don't like him," I responded. "But

in answer to your question, it is serious, and I don't know if we'll get married. It hasn't come up."

"I wouldn't say I don't like—" Flynn stopped and tapped my upper arm. "They're here."

We stood in a semicircle around the safe. It had felt a little odd as we trooped through Geoffrey's stateroom, or Bert Sand's stateroom, really. Lieutenant Binder had led the way. No one had talked since we'd reached the main deck.

Binder looked at each of us in turn. Me, Flynn, the real Geoffrey Bower, Seebold Frederickson, Jamie, and Officer Howland. "Mr. Bower, would you do the honors?"

Geoffrey stepped forward. Even though I'd only met Bert Sand once, it was hard for me to accept Cliff Munroe in the role. How were the crew members coping? Flynn had told Wyatt about Geoffrey's real identity with Genevieve and Maria Consuelo in the room. Word must be getting around to the rest of the crew. Everyone but Rick and Emil had known Sand as Bower.

"We've already checked for fingerprints," Lieutenant Binder said, nodding toward the safe. "Nothing useful."

Geoffrey pressed a long string of numbers on the keypad in a *clickety, clickety, clickety* rhythm. At last, there was a satisfying *thunk*. "It's open." Geoffrey stepped out of the way.

Jamie, wearing gloves, swung the door open. A purple velvet box sat on a pile of manila envelopes on a shelf at eye level. He reached for the case and took it down. We crowded closer as he opened it.

It was empty. The indentation of the big, black diamond showed on the velvet-covered platform inside, but there were no gems.

Binder was the first to speak. "Well, that's that."

Bower cleared his throat. "Excuse me, Lieutenant. I'd like to report a robbery."

Chapter 26

Flynn and I left the *Garbo* ahead of the others. Lieutenant Binder made it clear he had more questions for Bower and Frederickson. He asked us all to keep the theft of the Black Widow to ourselves.

Bert Sand's impromptu wake had grown and moved. The entire crew, along with Wyatt and Quentin, were gathered around several tables pushed together in the bar at Blount's. Wyatt was, as Flynn had said, a mess. Her hair was plastered to her cheeks by tears. But I understood why she wanted the company of the others. They'd all been deceived. Better to be with them, than sit alone in her room.

Flynn pulled a chair next to Genevieve's and held her hand. She gave him a wan smile that spoke of the emotional turmoil and tiredness of the past few days. I sat in an empty chair next to Rick.

The evening's conversation turned inevitably to the question of "Did you know?" Rick and Emil quickly admitted they did.

"You have duped me twice, my friend," Marius

said to Emil. "You persuaded me to work on this yacht, and you kept from me the real identity of the owner." He spoke with a smile, but there was an angry edge to his voice.

"I didn't know, but I suspected something was off," Genevieve said. "I asked him once if he liked the cuisine of the Greek isles and he said he'd never been there. I remember thinking, 'that is so weird,' because Rick had told me they'd sailed around Greece many times. But I put it down to misremembering or misspeaking because he was distracted."

Others chimed in with little slips Bert had made. Once it appeared he couldn't read a financial document Doug had asked him to review. Another time he said something to Maria Consuelo about 'his sister.' All of them claimed they had paused at the time, but then forgotten about it. But that's what humans did, wasn't it? If we were introduced to someone as so-and-so, we took that at face value. We created rational explanations for small anomalies, even if there were several over time. It took a big blow-up to reset our beliefs, and then we picked over everything in the past, examining it through a new lens.

"I was taken in completely," Ian claimed loudly. "I never had an idea."

The group switched to telling humorous, affectionate stories about Bert, and the table broke down into several small conversations. Rick leaned toward me. "Where have you come from?"

Binder had asked us not to tell anyone that the Black Widow was missing, so I told a partial truth. "Sergeant Flynn and I were with Mr. Frederickson and Mr. Bowers. The lieutenant is continuing his investigation."

Rick stiffened visibly, all the casualness of the prior question seeping away. "You and Genevieve's boyfriend—you are continuing your investigation too?"

Were we? With the revelations of the day, Genevieve and Wyatt were probably totally off the hook. And since the Black Widow was not in the safe, and since Geoffrey had not been Geoffrey after all, my theory about the reason for the poisoning and the theft also lay in a shambles. But I was unwilling to let it go, so I said, "Yes, we're still involved. Informally, of course."

He rose quickly from his chair. "I must speak to you. In private." He started toward the lobby. When I stood, Flynn shot me a curious glance across the table. I mouthed the word "Rick," and followed him out.

Rick was by the elevators. "We go to my room, please. I need your help."

The elevator doors opened, but I stepped backward. Go to his room? Was this a clumsy pass, or something more sinister? There was a killer, probably more than one killer, still on the loose. But then I spotted Flynn standing in the archway between the lobby and the bar. He nodded quickly. He was following. "Okay," I said to Rick. "Let's go."

Rick used the swipe card to unlock his door. His room was on the third floor, its furnishings exactly like the ones I'd glimpsed in Wyatt's room earlier in the evening. He stepped aside so I could go in first.

"No, you," I said, giving him a gentle shove. He went ahead and I followed. On the way in, I swung the lock guard across the opening to keep the door from closing. I heard the elevator ding behind us. Flynn, on his way, I was sure.

"Excuse." Rick went to the bureau and opened the top drawer. He rifled it briefly, his back was to me. When he turned around, the Black Widow was cradled in his hands.

"Rick! Where did you get that?" The words flew out involuntarily and loudly. Flynn banged through the door.

Rick looked from me to Flynn and back. "Please, please, you must help me."

Flynn went to the bathroom, emerging with a clean hand towel. "Give it to me. And the extra loose diamond too."

. "With pleasure." The moment he handed the Black Widow over, all the tension seemed to seep out of Rick's body and he was left exhausted and trembling. He pointed to the top drawer, where Flynn recovered the extra diamond.

"Where did you get the necklace?" I asked.

"I stole it. From the safe."

"Why did you take it?"

Rick collapsed into a desk chair in a movement so sudden Flynn put a hand out to stop him from bolting. But he wasn't going anywhere. He hung his head in his hands and began to sob. "It was an impulse. I shouldn't have taken it. Everything was changing. Mr. Bower was going to return to the ship. He was going to marry. Ms. Jayne would be taking over. Who knows if there was a place for me in this? I have worked for Mr. Bower for a long time. I thought to myself, don't I deserve something for all the hard work, the secret keeping? It has caused me much stress." He sighed. "So I thought, I will take the necklace. I will go back to Europe, and I will live a different life. A life on land."

"You knew the combination to the safe," Flynn suggested.

"Oh yes. Mr. Bower has opened the safe in front of me many times. It's a lot of numbers, but they play a tune, a tapping rhythm, I memorized long ago. Back when Mr. Bower lived on board, the real Mr. Bower."

"Why did you decide to tell me?" I asked. I tried hard to process what was happening. It was all too much, too fast.

"I regretted stealing it soon after I took it. Mr. Bower has been so good to me. I was going to put it back the next day, but then Bert was killed." He paused, hiccuping. "Then my problem was even bigger. I knew in no time the theft of the necklace would be seen as the motive for the murder. If I was caught with the necklace . . . I thought I could sneak it back in this morning, but the lieutenant said we would be watched the whole time. I have not slept. I cannot eat. I am so sorry for what I have done." He wiped his eyes with his thumbs. "You must believe me. I did not kill Bert."

"But you did steal a five-million-dollar necklace," Flynn said. "I'm a sworn officer of the law. Even though Julia and I did some investigating on our own,

I can't ignore the evidence of a crime. I'm going to call Lieutenant Binder now and tell him you have the Black Widow."

"I beg you. Please, tell him I did not kill anyone. Please."

"I know a great criminal lawyer," I said. "He'll be with you while you're questioned." Hadn't I made the same offer to Wyatt only a couple of days ago?

Flynn made a face at me, but I persisted, and each of us made our calls.

"What do you think?" Flynn asked me. We were on the familiar hard benches across from the receptionist's desk at the police station. Flynn on one and me on the other. Binder and Rick were on the other side of the door to the multipurpose room, waiting for my friend and lawyer, Cuthie Cuthbertson, who was on his way. The receptionist had gone home hours before. I didn't think there was anyone there besides the four of us and the firemen next door.

Lieutenant Binder had shown up five minutes after Flynn called and taken Rick into custody with a minimum of fuss. "What are you two doing here?" He didn't hide his annoyance. I opened my mouth to answer, but Binder interrupted. "Never mind. We'll talk after I've booked him. Come to the station. Wait for me." Blount's relieved-looking night manager had let us out a side door. They'd had their early season business disrupted too many times.

"I believe Rick," I told Flynn. "I think he took the necklace exactly as he said he did. He didn't kill Bert

Sand. Why would he? He knew the combination, and he knew Bert wasn't Geoffrey. You?"

"I don't see it," he agreed. "And who was his accomplice? Too many loose ends. I suspect the lieutenant will see it the same way."

"So we're back to square one," I said.

Flynn gave me a tired smile. "Don't despair. It's typical. I've ended up back there so often during this type of investigation, I bought furniture and turned square one into a bachelor pad." He paused, a frown wrinkling the skin over his nose. "Unless—"

"Unless what?" I sat forward on the bench.

"Unless you were right all along."

"How could I be right?" I threw my arms out in a gesture of defeat. "Rick did the theft and we agree he didn't do the murder. They're not connected."

Flynn pressed his point. "We know that, Julia. We know it now. But we didn't know it until half an hour ago. It's entirely possible the killers didn't know it either."

The glass door of the police station opened and the real Geoffrey Bower walked in. "The lieutenant called," he explained. "He said he has Rick in custody. He wants me to identify the Black Widow. As the owner," he clarified, reacting to the look I gave him. He sat on the bench next to me. "What are you talking about?"

Flynn hesitated, but I plunged in. "We don't think Rick killed Bert."

"Of course he didn't!" Geoffrey was vehement. "He stole from me because he was provoked. I put him in a terrible position. Rick would never hurt anyone, but especially Bert. They've shared the secret of my identity for the last few years. They joked together to blow off steam. It bonded them. I've seen it. Rick would never hurt Bert."

As Geoffrey spoke, I saw a gentle man, conflicted and plagued by guilt because he'd made a fortune off the suffering of others, a man who could fall in love like a teenager. A shy, socially awkward man who had never intended any harm.

Flynn must have seen something in him too. "Did Lieutenant Binder share with you Julia's theory of the murder?"

Geoffrey blinked. "Julia's theory? The lieutenant did say perhaps Bert was poisoned because the robbers thought he was me, and he would give them the combination to the safe in order to save his life. Of course, he didn't know the combination." Geoffrey's voice thickened with regret and grief. "Poor Bert. He landed what he thought was the role of a lifetime, and it got him killed. I got him killed."

"When the safe was empty, we thought Julia's theory was blown," Flynn told him. "But now we know the thief was Rick, and believe the loss of the necklace was unrelated to the poisoning. The killers didn't know the necklace wasn't in the safe. Julia's idea could still be the right one." He looked at each of us in turn, to see if we were following.

I was. "Following that logic, who would it have been?"

"It's easier to say who it wasn't," Flynn answered. Geoffrey was listening closely, his brow furrowed.

"It wasn't Genevieve. I'm her alibi," Flynn said.

"It wasn't Wyatt. Quentin and his parents are her alibi," I tagged onto his thought.

Flynn looked at me. "You're sure?"

I didn't hesitate. "Absolutely."

Geoffrey exhaled, a sigh of relief. He was in love with her. I'd almost forgotten. "It wasn't Rick, because he knew Bert wasn't me." He got into the spirit of it.

"Then it wasn't Emil, for the same reason," I said.

"Emil alibis Marius," Flynn said. "That leaves—"

"Doug and Ian," I almost shouted. "Neither knew Bert wasn't Geoffrey. Doug got Ian the job. They alibied each other for the time of the murder, but the police have only partially confirmed their whereabouts. They have the strength between them to dress and lift the corpse. And Doug, who may not have loved Bert, but certainly loved the *Garbo*, may have felt enough regret to clean up the scene."

"He wouldn't have wanted the mess sullying her," Geoffrey said. "In his precise way, Doug would have put things back to rights."

"But why now?" Flynn asked. "Why this week?"

"Even though Doug and Ian didn't know the secret, they knew things were changing. Wyatt was aboard and referring to Bert as her boyfriend," I said. "But I think the X factor was Ian. Ian is the new element. When they're together, it looks like Doug is the leader, but it's really Ian."

My friend, the criminal lawyer Cuthie Cuthbertson,

scurried by us with the briefest of nods and rapped on the door to the multipurpose room. "Cuthbertson."

Binder called, "Come in," and Cuthie disappeared into the inner sanctum.

When he'd gone, Flynn restarted our discussion. "Theories are fine, but we have no proof."

"They're the only pair who makes sense," I insisted.

"That's not proof."

"What if we could get it?" Geoffrey asked.

"Sure," Flynn said, "but how?"

Geoffrey leaned forward. "Bert didn't know the combination to the safe, but I do. If you wanted something so badly you'd kill for it, would you give up because of these crazy circumstances? What if someone offered you a second shot at the prize? The only people who know the Black Widow isn't in that safe are here in this building." He considered. "And Seebold, who's gone to bed."

"If your lawyer was here, he would tell you this isn't a good idea," Flynn cautioned.

"If my *friend* Seebold was here, he'd say the same," Geoffrey acknowledged. "But he's not, and I am, and I'm angry Bert's dead."

"Okay," Flynn replied. "Let's talk to the lieutenant."

We stood in the lobby of Blount's, at the archway leading into the bar. "Okay." Geoffrey stood up straight. "Showtime." During the time we spent figuring out the plan, I hadn't processed how difficult it would be for him to face the crew he'd deceived. And Wyatt even more so. "Has to be done sooner or later," he muttered, as if reading my thoughts. He strode into the room, hand out. They were all still there, much further into the evening's drinking.

"Hello, everyone. So wonderful to meet you all. Except, of course, Emil. We've met many times." Geoffrey gave them a hesitant smile. He went around the table, introducing himself and shaking hands. When he got to Wyatt, she jumped up and bolted from the bar.

Geoffrey looked after her sadly. His feelings for her hadn't changed.

"I'll go." Quentin followed her out. I didn't think he wanted to be around Geoffrey either.

Keep your head in the game, Geoffrey. Too much was riding on his performance.

He went to the bar and bought a round. "Please get my good friends here another of whatever they're drinking." Then he slipped into Wyatt's vacated chair. Flynn and I joined the gang as well, sitting on either side of Genevieve.

"I'm sorry about everything that's happened," Geoffrey told the group. "Especially, of course, about poor Bert. I hope you'll all consider staying on. I know everyone was excited about the refit."

The offer was met with silence. It seemed unlikely anyone would agree on the spot, but there was some nodding, some thoughtful faces.

"Sorry, man," Ian said. "Doug and I've already

signed on to another yacht. We leave first thing in the morning."

"I'm sorry to hear that," Geoffrey responded. "I hope there are no hard feelings."

The waitress brought the drinks. We helped her out, passing them across the table. I'd asked for a bottled beer, an empty glass, and an ice water. I lined them up in front of me, pouring half the beer into the glass. "The sergeant, Julia, and I were drinking over at Crowley's," Geoffrey told them. "Then I said, let's join the gang." He slurred the words slightly. I was surprised he was so good at playing the role, but then he'd been playing the role of Cliff Munroe for years.

The group got down to telling stories. Bert stories, *Garbo* stories, finally any boating story. The laughter was raucous, louder as the evening went on. Geoffrey took a couple of sips of his whiskey and slid it in my direction. I kept the glasses moving around the table, so it wasn't clear which glass was in front of him. He bought another round from the bar, and then another. At the other end of the table, Doug and Ian conferred in low voices. Doug shook his head twice, but Ian kept talking. My hopes rose.

Maria Consuelo surrendered first, saying her good nights. Genevieve walked her to her room and returned. "I see what you're doing," she whispered to me. "With the drinks."

"Can anyone else tell?" I whispered back.

"I don't think so."

The evening went on until we were the only customers left in the bar. Around us the waitresses cleaned

tables and folded cloth napkins for the next day. The
bartender yawned and looked at his watch.

Marius and Emil called it a night. "It has been an
experience," Marius said. I could tell Emil was reluc-
tant to leave. He was in charge of Geoffrey's safety,
but Geoffrey waved him off. "Get some rest, my man."

One last round, and Geoffrey lurched to his feet.
He signed the check and threw two hundred-dollar
bills on the table for the tip. "Time for nighty-night."

"Where are you staying?" Flynn asked him. "Did
you book a room here?"

"Nah." Geoffrey's voice was loud enough for
everyone in the almost empty barroom to hear. "I
had a room at a B&B across town, but I won't make
it that far. My boat's right here. I'm gonna sleep on
my boat." He staggered off in the direction of Blount's
back door.

Ian looked at Doug. "Time to turn in?"

"I think it is," Doug answered.

My stomach curled into a ball. Everything de-
pended on what happened now. Flynn waited until
Doug and Ian cleared the room, then stood. I stood
up too.

"Julia, no," Flynn commanded.

"I didn't come this far not to see this through," I
responded, but he had already left the bar. Genevieve
grabbed my hand and we crept into the silent, empty
lobby, then out the back door to the patio.

Below us, Geoffrey made a great show of weaving
his way toward the *Garbo*. The gangway was down,
and he shouted, "Honey, I'm home!" before he started

up. Somewhere, down there in the shadows, Flynn
waited.

Genevieve and I waited as well. "Flynn's a good
guy," I whispered to her.

She clutched my arm, shivering. "He is," she said.
"A good man at the wrong time."

"Look!" I caught my breath and pointed to the
dock. Two dark figures ran by, unidentifiable, even
under the lights. They started up the gangway after
Geoffrey. But as we watched, a third figure, larger
than the others, charged across the quay and tackled
one of men on the gangway. "Oomph!" The shout
could be heard across the water as the big man brought
the smaller man down.

Geoffrey yelled, "Emil! What are you doing?
You've spoiled it."

Then Flynn charged out of the darkness and tackled
the second man.

Lieutenant Binder, alerted by the noise, came out
on the main deck of the *Garbo*. "That's enough. Mr.
Merriman, Mr. Cowen, you are under arrest for tres-
passing. I have a number of things I'd like to discuss
with you at the police station." Then Jamie and
Officer Howland appeared on deck and handcuffed
Ian and Doug.

Emil apologized. "I'm sorry, I didn't know what
was happening. Looking after Mr. Bower is my job."

Chapter 27

I stood on the high ground in front of Windsholme, watching the *Jacquie II* come into dock with all the anticipation of a producer watching the curtain rise at a Broadway show. Today was the dress rehearsal, the gathering of close friends of the Snowden Family Clambake. Everyone was in his or her place: Sonny by the towering wood fire, Livvie in the kitchen, Mom in the gift shop. For the first time in years, everything felt right with the world. In two days the first boatload of tourists would arrive and the season would begin.

I hurried to meet our visitors. The JOATs—the Jacks of All Trades that served as the island's runners, bussers, and general support—were ahead of me, already helping people off the ship. The Snugg sisters came off the boat arm in arm with Gus's wife, Mrs. Gus. I'd invited the old curmudgeon himself, but nothing would tear him away from his restaurant at this time of year. "Can't stop to chat," Vee said as they passed. "Must claim our favorite table."

Emmy and Vanessa bounced down the dock, pushing Luther in a stroller. All three of them were smiling. "Thanks so much," Emmy said when she passed. "It's so generous of you to invite us to lunch. I'm glad I could get the day off." Vanessa ran off in search of Page. "Be careful!" Emmy called after her.

Binder, Flynn, and Chris disembarked together, an odd grouping. Both cops were in civilian clothes. I looked for Genevieve behind Flynn in the crowd, but didn't spot her. "What's happening with our friends?" I asked Binder when they reached the place where I stood.

"As soon as we got Mr. Cowen and Mr. Merriman to the station, they turned on each other like vicious dogs, each blaming the other, trying to duck the murder charge. They both have attorneys now. There will be some negotiating, but I'm confident we'll charge both of them with murder in the first." Chris gave me a quick hug and the three men moved on.

Quentin helped Wyatt off the boat and escorted her up the path that led by me. Even at a distance, I could see the purple circles under her eyes. She stopped and I looked directly at her, intending to convey my sympathy. Tears sprang to her eyes as she nodded her acknowledgment.

Back in the harbor, movers were off-loading everything from the *Garbo* that wasn't nailed down, preparing for her scheduled refit at Herndon's. To my surprise, Wyatt had committed to finishing the project. She and Geoffrey would work closely all summer. With time, would she get past his betrayal? I didn't think I could. I'd invited Geoffrey to the clambake. "Too many people." He'd shuddered. "Too soon. Maybe someday."

Captain George was the last one off the boat. He and his crew would have lunch at the clambake today, something they'd be unable to do for the rest of the season. "How'd it go?" I asked.

"Fine," he said. "They're good kids."

They were good kids, but they were kids. "They've got a good captain," I told him.

People had spread out over the island. They played boccie and volleyball on the great lawn, and lingered around the bar and the gift shop. As always, there was a group around the clambake fire, watching Sonny and his crew cook the meal under seaweed covered by tarps.

I walked back toward the dining pavilion, hugging myself. The day was perfect, the sun bright, the sky a cloudless blue. This was what I loved most about the Snowden Family Clambake—sharing Morrow Island with our guests. Windsholme was built as an exclusive retreat for a small family. My parents had made it available to thousands of people a year for the cost of a boat ride and a meal. Sharing was always better than hoarding.

I spotted Chris watching Page and Vanessa as they ran up the island hill. I went to him and he put an arm around me, hugging me to him.

"Have you asked Emmy about Vanessa's father?" I said.

"Not yet." He stepped back to look me in the eyes.

"I've applied to visit my brother in prison. That seems like the right first step."

"Good." I hugged him tight and then left him and headed back toward the dining pavilion. I had work to do.

On the way down the hill, I met Wyatt coming up alone. She greeted me with a hug. "Thank you for all you did for me this week."

I hugged her back. "I'm sorry it turned out the way it did, Wyatt."

She let me go. "And I'm sorry, Julia, for the way I treated you in high school. I've thought about it so often since. I was an unbelievable jerk back then."

"It's okay," I said. "Do you still see Lainey, Amber, and Melissa?"

She smiled for the first time in days. "We try. We're all so busy. Lainey's a pediatrician in Pittsburgh and—"

She continued on about her friends, where they lived and what jobs they held, but I didn't hear her. Lainey, a pediatrician. I had thought Lainey was stupid, and I was sure I'd never bothered to hide it. Maybe I was as guilty as they were. *Maybe we're all jerks in high school.*

From a discreet distance, I watched Mom in the gift shop, answering questions, chatting, taking money, giving change. My chest swelled and my throat constricted. Mom was back where she belonged, and Page and Jack would spend their childhood summers on the island, just as Livvie and I had, and as Mom had, and her mother before her, and back to Victorian times.

When the shop emptied, I stepped up to the counter. I could see baby Jack dozing in his portable crib in the corner, oblivious to the hubbub.

"Not many buyers on dress rehearsal day," Mom said. "But everyone seems to like the new merchandise." She spoke with such pride.

"I'd like to hire Emmy Bailey for one of the waitstaff openings," I said.

"That's a good idea."

"She can't keep doing double shifts at Crowley's. Not with her child care situation. She'd have to bring her kids out here with her to make it work."

Mom's brow creased. "Honey, I'm not sure I'm up to that. It will be hard enough to manage Jack if he happens to wake up cranky during prime shopping time."

"I know. I've thought of that. What if we hire a high school kid to watch all the children? You could supervise."

Her frown relaxed. "That would work. I think between you and me, Livvie, Sonny, and Emmy, we could keep enough of an eye."

The clambake staff would keep an eye on them too, if my own childhood was any indication. "I'm glad you think so."

I dropped in on Livvie in the kitchen. Of all my worries about opening, she and her cooks were the least of it. Though Livvie had only taken over the task the year before, the three other women were all pros with many years of experience putting out a big meal from the small kitchen. Livvie spotted me lingering in the doorway and gave a nod they were ready.

Standing under the pole that held the ship's bell that would call folks to lunch, I pantomimed to Sonny, asking if the lobsters were done He gave me the thumbs-up and I rang the bell.

The guests found their way back from wherever they'd been and settled at the picnic tables in the dining pavilion and scattered about the lawn. The waitstaff began running with cups of steaming clam chowder direct from the kitchen. The JOATs followed with pitchers of lemonade and iced tea for each table.

It went pretty well from my perspective. I was nervous because we were still short a few staff. Filling positions had been difficult in a tight summer job market. I kept my eye on the JOATs. Theirs was the entry-level job on the island; they were the newest and youngest. A couple of them did get confused about which tables they were assigned, and some groups ended up with four pitchers of drinks, others with none, but it was all cheerfully fixed by the waitstaff, or by the guests.

The bowls were cleared and the main course appeared—twin lobsters, steamed clams called steamers, corn, potato, onion, and an egg. From Livvie's kitchen the waitstaff brought containers of hot clam broth, melted butter, and bowls for shells.

And then the staff sat at the tables especially reserved for them. The dress rehearsal was the only time they would get to eat the clambake meal. After today, Livvie and her crew would serve a family-style meal of something delicious but inexpensive during the time between when the lunch guests left and the dinner guests arrived.

I circulated among the tables, feeling so lucky to have so many of our regular employees return. On any other day, tourists would be asking for my help, and I'd show them how to dredge the clams in the hot broth to clean them, or how to use a nutcracker to get the tasty meat from the lobster's claws. But today's guests were lobster-eating pros, as the almost silent crowd attested, intent on their meals.

Le Roi circulated too, winding around the guests' ankles, waiting for the inevitable lobster treats snuck to him under the table. He was back on his island, truly the king.

I spotted Lieutenant Binder at a table with Quentin and Wyatt. There was a fourth tray on the table, with a barely eaten lobster, but Flynn wasn't with them.

I found him on the cliffs on the north side of the island, facing the mouth of the outer harbor. I went and stood next to him, hating to intrude, but also hating to neglect a friend in need.

"She's gone." He kept his eyes on the horizon.

"I'm sorry. Where?"

"Flying to Jacksonville to be the private chef on another yacht. The seafaring life has hijacked her."

"I think it's the sense of family she gets from being part of the crew." I realized as soon as the words came out of my mouth I was saying the life she'd created with Flynn hadn't been enough for her. "And the adventure," I added.

He didn't say anything, just stared out at the horizon.

The poor man. I looped my arm through his and stood with him. I thought he'd pull away, but he didn't. We'd come a long way from the beginning of our relationship. Finally, he said, "Let's go back."

I helped clear the trays and dump the shells. Every piece of garbage we created had to come off the island with us. Livvie's cooks sent out blueberry grunt swimming in vanilla ice cream and everyone sat down again.

I took my dessert to Mom's table, ready to dig in, but she motioned me to follow her. We walked up to Windsholme and stood outside the ugly, orange fence. There was a commotion on the long front porch. Page and Vanessa ran up and down it, screaming, "The ghost! The ghost! We saw her!"

"Girls!" Mom projected to be heard over their shouting. "Come away from there. It's dangerous."

The sound of her voice brought me back to my own childhood. I'd heard those words when she ordered Livvie and me off that porch. The mansion, closed up and abandoned, had been forbidden to us too. Then it had only been dangerous because it was neglected. Now it was also damaged by fire.

Page and Vanessa had stopped running and were slowly making their way to the gap in the fence.

"I'm going to pay Wyatt's firm to do the architectural study," Mom said. "We're going to fix up Windsholme."

I'd been opposed to the project, yet strangely, I felt a weight lift off me. "Will you restore or renovate?"

"Renovate," she answered.

"Really?" That was a surprise. "Do you plan to live there in the summer?"

"Maybe," she answered. "In an apartment upstairs. But I want to renovate to realize your dream—to add wedding receptions, and corporate retreats, and other events to the clambake. The business is supporting three families now, not one. We need to expand."

I stood, openmouthed. It was a brilliant solution. "Earlier today, I was thinking that the best thing about Morrow Island is sharing it," I told her.

"Exactly." Mom put her arm around me and leaned in for the hug. Page and Vanessa danced around us.

"I love you, Mom," I said. "I love *this*."

Recipes

Tarragon Ricotta Gnocchi
with Lobster Velouté

The yacht Garbo *is in Busman's Harbor, Maine, so naturally lobster is on the menu. The velouté was one of the signature dishes at Genevieve's Portland restaurant, which is why it tastes so familiar to Julia.*

Ingredients for the Gnocchi

1 16-ounce container ricotta
¾ cup Parmesan cheese
¾ cup Romano cheese
¼ teaspoon salt
⅛ teaspoon pepper
2 eggs, beaten
¾ cup all-purpose flour
1 Tablespoon fresh tarragon, finely chopped

Ingredients for the Velouté

3 Tablespoons butter
3 Tablespoons flour
1½ cups lobster stock
⅓ cup heavy cream
4–6 ounces cooked lobster, chopped

fresh tarragon or parsley for garnish

Instructions

Heat oven to 350 degrees. Boil and salt 4–6 quarts of water in a pot. Grease a small baking dish with butter.

In a bowl, stir together the ricotta, grated cheeses, salt, pepper, and eggs. Stir in the flour in ¼-cup helpings until it reaches the consistency of a sticky dough. Using a tablespoon, drop rounded spoonfuls into the boiling water. When the gnocchi rise back to the top of the water, cook for about a minute more, then remove to the baking dish using a slotted spoon.

In a saucepan over medium heat, melt the butter. Add the flour and stir together to create a roux. Cook for 1 to 2 minutes being careful to not allow the roux to brown. Whisk in the stock and cook until the velouté coats the back of a spoon. Stir in the cream and the lobster meat and cook for one minute more. Keep warm.

Pour ½ cup of the velouté over the gnocchi, reserving the remainder in the pan. Put the gnocchi in the oven and bake for 15 to 20 minutes, until the sauce is barely bubbling.

To serve, put a puddle of the reserved velouté on a plate. Add 3 to 4 gnocchi and garnish. Serve immediately.

Serves 4.

Herbed Halibut Sous-Vide

Genevieve cooks the halibut to perfection using a sous-vide device. While they were once very pricey and therefore used only by professional chefs, sous-vide devices are now far more affordable for home cooks.

Ingredients

1½ pounds halibut filet at least 1-inch thick
2 Tablespoons chopped dill
2 Tablespoons chopped chives
4 Tablespoons softened butter, divided
½ Tablespoon lemon zest
juice from a large lemon
salt
pepper

Instructions

Following the instructions for your *sous-vide* device, fill a pot of water and set the temperature to 105 degrees F. Bring the water up to temp.

Cut the fish into four individual portions. Rub each portion with ½ Tablespoon butter, then sprinkle with salt and pepper. Spread ½ Tablespoon dill and ½ Tablespoon chives over each portion.

Put each portion in a zipper-sealable plastic bag and lower into the water, sealing at the last possible moment so the water pushes the air out of the bag. Or, you can vacuum seal the bags using the "moist" setting, if you have the proper equipment.

Set the timer for 35 minutes.

When the timer goes off, remove the fish from the bags and reserve any juices that have accumulated.

Heat a large frying pan over medium high heat. Melt the remaining 2 Tablespoons of butter and stir in the lemon zest. Add the fish and sear quickly, about 1 minute per side. Add the lemon juice and accumulated juices to the pan and cook 1 minute longer.

Put fish on a warmed platter and pour the sauce over. Serve with lemon wedges.

Serves 4.

Oven-Roasted Beer-Can Chicken with Roasted Potatoes

Livvie makes this dinner when her mother calls an impromptu family meeting. It's a quick meal that pleases any crowd. Often, Beer-Can Chicken is made on the barbecue with indirect heat, but Sonny is the griller in the family, and Livvie knows he won't be back from Morrow Island until late, so she makes it in the oven. While Livvie cooks it using an actual beer can, you can purchase a device called a beer can chicken holder from almost any kitchenware vendor.

Ingredients for the Chicken

1 whole chicken, 4 – 4½ pounds
12-ounce beer can—any brand you have on hand
     will do
olive oil for rubbing over the chicken
Livvie's rub for the chicken (or substitute your
     own rub)

Livvie used the following ingredients for the rub:

2 Tablespoons kosher salt
½ Tablespoon black pepper
1 Tablespoon paprika
1 Tablespoon dried oregano
½ Tablespoon ground coriander
½ Tablespoon garlic powder
½ Tablespoon onion powder

½ Tablespoon cumin
1 teaspoon jalapeno powder (optional)
½ teaspoon lemon zest
½ teaspoon lime zest

Instructions

Preheat oven and sheet pan to 400 degrees. Stir together rub ingredients. Rinse chicken and pat dry. Rub chicken all over, inside and out, with olive oil. Rub chicken all over, inside and out, with the rub mix. Open beer can and pour out or drink 4 ounces, leaving 8 ounces in the can. Stand chicken on beer can by placing the neck over the can. Place on a rimmed baking sheet. Roast in oven for 1 hour.

Ingredients for the Potatoes

2 – 2½ pounds fingerling potatoes
olive oil
salt
black pepper
dried oregano
garlic
2 Tablespoons chopped fresh cilantro

Instructions

Cut potatoes into ½-inch pieces. Toss with olive oil and seasonings. When chicken is done, remove from baking sheet pan and place on platter. Toss potatoes with drippings left in sheet pan and roast 20 to 25 minutes.

Serves 6 to 8.

Acknowledgments

The Age of the Ship is long over, but in Maine it remains closer to us than in many other places. Ships, from warships to mega-yachts to beautiful sailboats to wooden boats, are built in Maine, contributing to the economy and the vibrancy of the coast. As I wrote this book, I was amused by how many of our normal, everyday terms come to us from our ancestors' dependence on boats, and how deeply that past is embedded in each of us.

Two books steered me through the world of super-yachts and mega-yachts. *The Insiders' Guide to Becoming a Yacht Stewardess*, by Julie Perry, was an invaluable resource, chock-full of colorful anecdotes and practical advice. *Mediterranean Summer,* by David Shalleck with Erol Munuz, gave me a good sense of the challenges and rewards of Genevieve's life aboard the *Garbo.*

I would like to thank the usual crew, who keep me focused and writing. First and foremost, my writers' group, to whom this book is dedicated. Thank you also to the Wicked Cozy Authors, including Maddie Day, Jessica Ellicott, J. A. Hennrikus, Liz Mugavero, with a special shout-out to Sherry Harris, who once again provided valuable feedback while working on her own addition to the Sarah Winston Garage Sale Mysteries. Thanks, as always, to the Maine Crime Writers, especially to Kaitlyn Dunnett, Kate Flora, and Lea Wait.

A big thank-you to everyone at Kensington for their tremendous support for the Maine Clambake series, especially my editor, John Scognamiglio, Karen Auerbach, Robin Cook, and cover artist Ben Perini. And a special thank-you to my agent, John Talbot.

Finally, to my family, who have been endlessly supportive and loving: Rob Carito, Sunny Carito, Viola Carito, Kate Donius, and Luke Donius, and especially to my husband Bill Carito who creates the Maine Clambake series recipes. Thank you from the bottom of my heart.

Connect with Us

Visit us online at
KensingtonBooks.com
to read more from your favorite authors, see books
by series, view reading group guides, and more.

Join us on social media

for sneak peeks, chances to win books and prize packs,
and to share your thoughts with other readers.

facebook.com/kensingtonpublishing
twitter.com/kensingtonbooks

Tell us what you think!

To share your thoughts, submit a review,
or sign up for our eNewsletters, please visit:
KensingtonBooks.com/TellUs.